Of Hawks and Sparrows

Of Hawks and Sparrows

Collected Stories and Poems

SATABDI SAHA

PARTRIDGE

A Penguin Random House Company

To order additional copies of this book, contact
Partridge India
000 800 10062 62
www.partridgepublishing.com/india
orders.india@partridgepublishing.com

CONTENTS

Dedicated to my late parents

ACKNOWLEDGEMENTS

To Basab Bijayee Guha for his inspiration, help and guidance.
To my nephew Debanu Das for typing my manuscript with care.
To my departmental colleagues and specially to Prof. Anuradha Ghosh
for motivating me to writing my first story.
To my family for their technical assistance and support.

PART I

STORIES

WHAT REMAINS

She brought the sun in my bones. Inside the damp room I stopped shivering. Dress torn, hair dishevelled, her eyes pierced the dark with a light, born of dreams. That night, like every other night, she woke me up. Sitting on a stool she looked at me imploringly, or so I thought, and then vanished. Getting down from the bed I opened the windows. The street lamps were disturbingly vulgar on the open drains and pot-holes. A clutch of dark lay huddled beyond; on the sidewalks, drenched with the night-sweat of the city. I wondered where she had gone. What was the street like where she lived, what kind of house that took her in, her friends, or did she have any? Standing by the window, the stench of drains was invading my consciousness like a day gone bad with stains of pain. I recalled the moment she came to me, face wet, yet with a sparkle of expectancy in her eyes. I thought that my action on that particular day was consistent with the logical sanctity of my own reasons. I remembered to have walked back lightened somehow. She loved me. Yet I lacked the courage to accept it then.

Thirty five-year old, I was working in a private company; independent, but slowly draining out the cold heat of dwindling youth in a cramped two-roomed flat in the back-streets of Calcutta. My aunt and uncle with their two adult boys lived in a two-storeyed house, just a minute's walk from my hole. Although my income was modest, I could easily afford to provide for one or even two dependants. I lost my parents by the time I was thirty and at times felt the fear of white-walled emptiness throttling me in the night. There was no question of abjuring the unhindered freedom I love-hated so much. Often, to dispel my boredom I went to my uncle's house nearby where I was not unwelcome.

Most of the rooms in my uncle's house were let. My aunt, a woman who lived only to count coins, was obsessively domineering. Under her ever-observant eyes, uncle basked in inactive bliss. Her idea of taking care of his health meant piling his plate with food whenever there was an opportunity. Uncle, in return for this favour, remained oblivious of her habit of terrorizing the victims unfortunate enough to incur her wrath. In his heart of hearts he considered her to be a harridan who needed appeasing by bootlicking servitude. He thought it safer to seek refuge under her strong clutch than contradict her in any way. She was the mistress of the house and had the last say about everything under the sun. Aunt was a freewheeling malevolence with whom her sons too compromised; but it was only a subtle exploitation, for their own parochial gains. She slaved for them, making the two absolutely useless and bone-lazy. Continuously on the run, she was always shopping, banking, and busy with outdoor jobs as well as the household chores. Even though I knew what she was, I could not help pitying her. After all one couldn't deny her devotion to her family which took full advantage of it. I talked to her on this several times.

'Aunt, why don't you tell your boys to run errands for you?'

'No, I can't. You know how they slave the whole week in colleges and libraries and what not!'

'But you're growing old, aunt!'

'To be sure I am!'

'Then keep a servant.'

'Oh! We can't afford the luxury', she said with a meaningful glance at me, 'considering we're all dependent on your uncle's pension and a pittance as rent.' I was silenced.

It was at my uncle's place that I first met Disha. She was then a mere child of about twelve, plump and physically mature for her age. People could easily mistake her for fifteen. Yet there was such a naiveté in her looks that one could not seriously rate her more than only a seven or eight year-old girl. What struck me, apart from the rustic look of her's, were her dark wide-apart eyes and a tiny rose-bud mouth so unusual among rural Indian children. With those two striking features I could identify her from a thousand faces. Disha had gripped my soul.

'Here, look, a new mouth to feed,' said my aunt, pushing her towards me.

'Who's she?'

'My elder sister got a brood of them in Midnapur. Can't feed them though. But every year, a bellyful. Now she's sent this one to me, to be my torment. As it is, none in this house cares a fig for how I work, day in and day out, and here comes another!'

'Just a baby,' I said.'

'Baby, my foot! Big enough to turn the heads of young men! Charwoman now, and then a watch dog! Oh! Why has god sent this curse to me!'

'Aunt, stop, stop I say! Have you gone mad?'

'I shall be,' she howled, 'and soon!'

Little Disha looked on in terror. In aunt's blazing eyes and crooked mouth, she saw a predatory malignancy. Her lips twitched and tears described the latent terror that slashed her mind and soul. Aunt had found another victim.

There sprouted an intuitive liking between Disha and me. With searing pain I watched her often, so lonely and dejected, at my uncle's house. A pre-cognitive kinship, a kinship between two loners hankering after a miraculous destination, brought us close to each other. In those very rare moments, I came to know that she sorely missed her home, her siblings, her parents, and her school. The family bond was strong, strong enough to endure hardship and poverty for years, until one day her father, a factory worker fell seriously ill. Disha, the second of the elder daughters was old enough to be sent away to people who would assuredly take care of her, while the eldest looked after the house and the other siblings when their mother replaced her husband in the factory. I tried to cheer up Disha in vain. City life, food, T.V. didn't help to bring the sparkle in the child's eyes. The sullenness enraged my aunt even more.

Sometimes on week-days when I went to work, Disha would be walking along the road with a shopping bag in hand, or a bundle of clothes tucked under her arm. Her face grew tanned, hair dry and rough, as she ran errands several times a day. One day I caught her on the street and asked her about school.

'School, what school Didi?' (sister)

'Why, don't you study in a school? There's Shishu Vidyayatan near your house!'

'Aunt said, admissions are not on.'

'May be so, because you've come in the middle of the session. But surely you can repeat your lessons at home now.'

Disha was silent. After a while she said, 'Yes. But I am weak in sums. Will you teach me at your house? I can come to you with the books I have brought with me, can't I Didi?' she asked eagerly, facing me. I demurred. I generally came home after ten at night, was too tired even to eat, let alone teach Disha.

'Yes, I mumbled, but what about your brothers? Surely they can teach you, can't they?' Disha's eyes clouded, mouth twitched. She didn't utter another word and looked away. I, in my turn looked at my scarred and empty rib-cage. Was it really so difficult for me to decide?

Gradually the holes on Disha's dresses grew big. Her eyes, once so lustrous, deadened with exertion. Washing, dusting, and shopping. Her hungry look, unbuttoned my tightened fears, making me wake up nights; my hideous face staring at the darkness within me. In the mirror I saw myself. Two different faces appeared. One, I did not recognize. The other, was horrible! So many eyes! They appeared on the wrong places. And with a shock I saw dead eyes, fish eyes! I screamed in terror! They were melting. Melting, trickling down my dress. I dared not look anymore. I felt myself disintegrating. Rushing to my bed, I tried to sleep in vain.

Aunt complained that Disha often came late from her errands. Her glances developed a furtiveness I was anxious to overlook. I pleaded with aunt, not to send her out on the streets, but to no avail. Aunt's arthritis seemed to intensify greatly after Disha's arrival. The latter worked as a slave merely to survive.

By the third month of her arrival, I observed the girl's bruises with concern. On her cheeks, the telling pink-blue maps; the hands hardened, streaked eerie red-purple, and near the elbows and arms darkness had made its unholy presence. Still I didn't speak out. I made myself forget the mirror episode.

Thunderstorms lashed the city that day. Calcutta was literally drowning. I managed to hail a taxi and head home early. As I reached the stairs, I heard a feral like whining. Looking up at the stairwell I saw Disha. She was soaked through and through and looked at me like a hunted animal.

'Didi, she wept, please let me stay with you!'

'Disha you've run away!'

'Yes, they all started beating me!'

'Who?'

'Everyone. Uncle too!'

'What did you do?' I asked, climbing the staircase with her.

'Broke a plate. Aunt told me to hurry up,' said she, her words choking with hiccups;—'I tried to, and it broke. I didn't do it deliberately Didi, I really didn't.'

'Hmm.' I was enveloped in flames.

'I won't go there anymore Didi! I want to stay with you!'

I mounted the second floor and opened the door of my flat. 'But you must, they must be looking for you! I'll take you there with me.'

'No, no, no, please Didi, let me stay with you, please! I promise I won't bother you. I'll wash your clothes, even cook for you; please Didi!'

I didn't answer; I was concerned about my losing face with my relatives for harbouring a truant child. I ought to do what was right. Restore her to her guardians, and give them a piece of my mind for their treatment of her. No imploring of the girl could shake me. I believed in righteousness. Prudish? No, not at all! I took out an old dress, too big for her, a towel, and told her to dry and change. Her face shone instantly with gratitude. Wiping her tears she smiled. I averted my face. After dinner Disha waited expectantly for me to tell her where she was to sleep. Her hiccups had vanished. There was silence. She sat huddled on the bed, eyes heavy with relentless crying. The rain fell in drizzles. The street lamps glowed wet, the pot-holes still overflowed. The stench of drains floated, fierce and strong. Taking out an umbrella, I held the child's hand, locked the door and went out. There wasn't a street-dog to be seen that night. I felt Disha's hand tremble in mine as we moved on. When we reached my aunt's house it was menacingly dark though it was only nine o' clock. I knocked, the door opened and I saw my aunt's shocked face. Promptly handing over Disha to her, I walked on. I didn't look back. Didn't look back anymore.

Sunday morning. I visited aunt. I was surprised to find her sitting, watching T.V. with uncle. The boys were out as usual. She had a relaxed look. I asked her about the child.

'Can't be found', she answered, placidly chewing betel leaves.

'What? When? Where did she go?' Blood spilt inside me.

'The very first thing I saw in the morning was that she was not in the house.' She replied curtly.

'But have you informed the police?'

'Police? Who has the time for it?'

'But aunt, she's your niece!'

'So what! I have not signed a bond that I'll have to look for someone who chooses to run away!'

'But it's wrong; you just can't let a child go away like this!' I gasped for breath.

'Oh! Don't be so naive! You know she's been mixing with local boys don't you!'

'All the more reason you should protect her since she is like your daughter!' I lost my cool.

'Daughter, my foot! Thrust inside my throat like a cork, to choke me to death, that hussy! Cunning as a fox, black as the devil! Drove the hell out of me, these three months, that slut! Showing herself to be neglected to everyone out on the streets! That's where she'll end up, take my word for it!' She gesticulated fire. Uncle sat listening, swimming placidly on the hot waters of her wonderful vocabulary!

'Aunt how could you say such things! I'll go to the police station, now, to lodge a diary.'

She jumped up. 'You'll do no such thing!' she countered nonchalantly. 'I know where she's gone. One of the local boys, I won't tell you his name, I knew, had taken a fancy to her. I arranged everything. He and his friends came and the rest was quietly managed.'

'When?' My heart lost a beat.

'That night when you brought her back.'

I couldn't speak. Something whipped me inside. I sank to my knees, lacerated, bleeding. In between my sobs floated the night; that drenched night when Disha came to me for the last time.

KINSHIP

Richa stood waiting for forty-five minutes under the sun to catch a bus. The sky had burst into a flame of betrayal. She felt she was worse off than a stray dog in a shade. Generally Richa took her own car to school, a ten or fifteen minutes' drive. But that day it was different. Everything, even the car, which wouldn't budge in the morning, connived to make her day a disaster. To think of walking at least an hour in the heat, made her weak in the knees. She looked around hopefully. No, not even rickshaws in sight. Cursing herself she ambled along, scalded and beaten to the bones.

The day had begun on a wrong note. The car refused to start, no matter how hard she tried. Exasperated, Richa took a bus to school only to hear the terrifyingly numbing news of her student's death. It crumpled her inside like a piece of paper. Then the condolence meeting and the school closing early. Her student, her favourite pupil. He wasn't any more. She stopped, looked vaguely and began to walk. Her stomach turned as the deadly heat burnt into her flesh, preventing a brisk walk. Ambling along without an umbrella seemed to be a nemesis, she thought, for an unrecognized sin she might have committed. The day's claws were poised to tear her apart. At last she reached her destination. But the ordeal was far from over. The lift too, she realized with a shock, was out of order.

The climb through the unusually steep stairs to the third floor was sheer cruelty. It generally was, but that day it drained her dry. Panting hard near the door, she thirsted for a glass of ice-cold water, but the maid, infernally sluggish after a siesta was late as usual to answer the bell. But in spite of her suffering, a sigh of relief escaped Richa's lips as she entered her lavishly decorated flat. The unforeseen trials and tribulations of the day seemed unreal at that moment. But the feeling was transitory. She switched on the bedroom fan; it rotated for a second and then stopped. There was a power cut. A blind fury enveloped her. No use relaxing. She went to the washroom to cool herself.

As she showered, Richa recalled the day's events. It was impossible to reconcile herself to what had happened. Listless, she walked inside the bedroom. Newspapers she hadn't touched were lying on the bed. Cursorily she leafed through them. Inside her head was a continuous whirlwind. In the empty teachers' lounge, she had sat with her hands on her cheeks, unable to figure things out. The boy had attended class yesterday; there was always a smile on his chubby face. Eyes closed, she tried to remember . . . .

Unbelievable. Unbelievable that she was still alive while the boy . . . no she couldn't. She couldn't go for the last farewell like the others. In a flash the face of her son appeared. Richa hankered after the warmth of her son's bear hugs but he was far away at that time.

The cell-phone rang. An unknown number. A male voice asked her name and introduced himself as an employee of the bank she had taken a loan from, to buy a house. The caller insisted on a visit, to verify her address. Richa annoyed, was in no mood to comply. Fatigue was taking over. But the voice was importunate. It only took seconds to realize that refusal would mean delay in paperwork and consequently sanctioning of the loan. She acquiesced. Time passed. The day's calamity appeared in bits and pieces, punctuating the tedious wait for the man. Each recollection of her pupil created piercing wounds, the pain underlining the irretrievable loss she would have to confront in class everyday and perhaps for a long time. But irritation got the better of her. The caller had assured her that he would certainly arrive within fifteen minutes. Still there was no sign of him, though nearly an hour had elapsed. Lunch was postponed. Richa sighed as she closed the windows to ward off the searing heat outside. Suddenly, through the glass window she saw a man entering the housing complex. It must be the bank employee, she surmised. The wait was insufferable. He needed to be given a piece of her mind for making her suffer in this heat. But all her resentment vanished when the door was opened. The plight of her visitor could not invite the remonstrance she wished to spew out a while ago. He was a teenager of nineteen or thereabouts, completely soaked with perspiration, a handkerchief tied to his head, panting with exhaustion and apologizing for arriving late. Richa ran and switched on the fan, which to her delight was working. The maid was ordered to bring a cold drink for the visitor.

Vicariously suffering, she offered him a towel which he politely refused. He then took out the handkerchief from his head and wiped his face, astonished at the reception from the lady of the house. Her patience gave him time to recover. Unaccustomed to walking in the gruelling heat, Richa had felt the agony that very day. She urged the boy to drink the lemonade.

'Thank you ma'am, I'll have it a little later. Would you please give me an address proof?'

'At present there isn't any, since we shifted to this flat only a month ago and have yet to get our new residential address on ration cards, electricity bill etc. They are in progress however.'

'But ma'am you'll have to furnish me with some proof of your residence here. A gas-receipt perhaps?'

'May be, but I'll have to look for it.'

The receipt was unavailable even after rummaging through the drawers.

'Sorry I can't provide you with any kind of receipt right now.'

'But it won't do. You'll have to give me some proof.'

'I know, but what can I do! Perhaps I may have a word with your manager and tell him about my problem. Will you give mc his number?'

The boy rang up his direct superior. 'I am at Lyons Range, Mr. Roy. No sir, I've not received any document. She says, she won't give any'.

It was a lie. A blatant lie. After the conversation, she exploded. 'I didn't give you! How could you say that?'

'Yes, you didn't give me any address proof. Is it a lie?'

'That is different. Did I tell you I won't give you any? Didn't you see that I tried to find one? After making me wait for nearly an hour without lunch, you're lying and for no reason at all! Is this how you behave with your clients?'

'Look madam, I've got to do a job. I need an address proof. I have been sent here for this purpose only.'

'Very well, but why did you lie to Mr. Roy?'

'I only told him you couldn't furnish any proof. Is it a lie?'

'Yes it is. Because you didn't say 'couldn't' but 'didn't'. I'll definitely complain against you for this behaviour!'

'How have I misbehaved?'

'You have lied about me, that's how'.

'I didn't mean to . . . . please ma'am I'll lose my job . . . .' Richa's face hardened. Too infuriated to reply, she kept mum. The boy's face was blanched with fear. He trembled inside. Richa looked impervious to any kind of pleading. She was all stone and rock. The soggy earth quickly dried up by the latent heat of unbridled rage. He still made an effort.

'Ok. I'll report that your address in genuine. Only don't complain, please madam!' With a face shrivelled with agony, he walked to the door, wiping his moist face. The drink was still on the table. Richa's eyes flashed on it for a second, bearing no impact whatsoever. Fuming, she refused to give it a thought. Nor could she provide any excuse for this gesture of hers. Disorientation. She tried giving it a satisfactory name. He was gone. The drink stood staring at her face. Vanity. The drink was still there. Ego? Yes. There was no playing hide and seek anymore. The boy, a fledgling, a mere child, a little older than the pupil she lost!

Food tasted unusually bitter at lunch, though she was ravenous. Images of her son without a head-gear, rushing from door to door would come. It left her shivering. Minutes ticked by, Richa gradually fell asleep. She dreamt of her pupil with his hands tied with a handkerchief, then a station, a boy waiting for the last train—blurred faces, the heat, and she herself, looking for something lost, jostled, pushed by people, many people. Sleep came in fits and starts. The silent, eerie hall, interspersed by a bluish haze, then again a thin spiky-haired face in a school uniform reaching for the water bottle. The teachers' lounge, an overturned chair, an empty glass; confusing, so confusing. Hands pointing. Several hands with twisted nails pointing at her. In the fading light she lay in a maze of headgears and handkerchiefs, pulling her down, pulling her down. She woke up with a start.

Richa opened the windows to let in the cool air outside. For several minutes she sat staring at her son's photograph. Then she fetched herself a glass of water and sat down on the bed. From the window she could see the fading light outside. On the manicured garden the last streaks of the melting sun topped the leaves. In the crawling darkness of the courtyard she saw two shapes. They grew gigantic and more gigantic until she could bear no more. A distilled vision of a lemon coloured bottle seemed to overwhelm her. Gradually she relaxed. Her face took on a determined look. Richa picked up her mobile. Then she pressed the 'received' button. Her fingers trembled and simultaneously a rebellion surged inside her, but she quelled it. Her heart beat fast as she pushed the callers' list. There was a tinkle at the other end, and then a voice. She was right. It was the same boyish tone, unmistakably.

THE HOME-COMING

Aditi rested her frail hands on the arm-chair and looked outside. The sky was cloudy and a slight drizzle had begun. It was pleasant to think that summer was finally over and monsoon had arrived. She was about to resign herself to the balmy coolness of the breeze, when a sudden stench invaded her nostrils. The heat-toasted garbage that was littered outside her ground-floor flat, was disturbed by just a smattering of droplets, the moisture unsealing the latent malodour that circled in great sweeps in the neighbourhood. It was impossible to stay still any more. She lifted the end of her sari to her nose, got up, and flopped down on the bed. It was no use. For thirty years the pollution had become a part of her existence. Living in a cramped two-roomed rented apartment amidst shanties and open drains, she did not expect anything different. It was her destiny of choice. She drifted unconsciously to her maiden days. No matter how much she tried, it was impossible to bridle the nostalgia which invaded most of her hours in bed. Aditi found it odd that even after years of marital fulfilment the memories of her father's house haunted her again and again.

It was a shocking discovery to her friends and relatives that Aditi, the beautiful daughter of Suren Chatterjee was engaged to a motor-mechanic. When reprimands failed, restrictions were imposed on her movements. Her father's huge bungalow became a prison. Aditi hated the opulence and the luxury of physical comfort. It seemed claustrophobic. She cried bitterly for freedom.

Finally Aditi eloped, married and came to live in the two-roomed dingy flat with Robin. But that's another story. Thirty years of struggle had divergent effects on her life. For her the consoling fact was that her son who was given the best education lived up to her expectation. Initially Aditi took up teaching in the nearby slums to augment the family income. Her relentless slaving had paid off. Rudra had a good job, good enough to run the family, but years of unmitigated toil had a negative impact on her health. She was suffering from bouts of pain in her stomach which left her drained of strength.

Often, when the pain subsided, she lay exhausted on the bed, thinking of the house she had once lived. A splendid one, with a front garden, overlooking the main road. Her own room was spacious, with costly upholstery and dolls which her father often bought for her when he returned from abroad. These reminiscences made her feel guilty but they were like vents to psychic freshening up which she needed in that two-roomed hole in a filthy Beliaghata area where life had come to a halt. The cramped dark room where she lay, was stifling. Aditi swiftly brushed aside those thoughts and stared at the packages. A sense of well-being was dominant whenever she looked at the packed boxes in her room. They were going to leave the flat at last. Robin had finally built a one-storeyed house in Bansdroni. They had saved every rupee for it and had deprived themselves of many comforts at the height of their youth. Aditi dreamed of going to her new house within a month or so. She had often gone to supervise the building, instructing the labourers, sketching, drawing, designing. Her own house. A thrill ran through her, thinking that the time was nearly ripe for them to move. She was sure to recover quickly. Imagining the rows of flower-pots on the balcony, open to the south, letting in uninhibited air; the field in front and little boys playing, was so exhilarating! She herself had chosen the plot of land though it cost her more than she had expected. But then, it was her dream!

Aditi adored her husband, though there were squabbles, very trivial in nature.

'Diti, what's wrong with you? Why don't you freshen up in the evenings?'

'I don't have time to preen myself like a peacock'. Her voice screeched with irritation.

'Do you know that the house-maid comes better dressed than you?'

'I don't care. I just don't feel like dressing up in this filthy house and in this filthy place'. A shadow of pain a contorted Robin's face.

'Diti you have chosen to live with me. I know I am poor and don't have the means to provide you with what you deserve. I shouldn't have brought you to this life of penury!'—Aditi was ashamed of herself. How on earth could she say this to Robin! She could not deny that this involuntary reaction was the fall'-out of the suppressed longing for her father's house. Anguish and guilt pervaded her.

'Forgive me, Robin, I never meant to complain. I know how much you slave, just to make me happy! I promise I'll dress up nicely every evening.'

'Will you?' Robin hugged his wife, with fervour.

Lying sick in bed she recalled the moments with her husband. Their quarrels, intimacies and the mutual respect and love they felt for each other.

Aditi dragged herself from the bed. The maid had gone. So much was still left to be done. She was unable to fathom what disease sapped her of her strength. The doctors said that it was gastric ulcer. But how long does an ulcer take to heal? It was quite unpleasant lying in the bed with so much work unfinished in the new house. Strange, that Robin who was so keen on moving, had become insouciant so suddenly. He was away most of the time, doing odd jobs while Rudra stayed at home to look after her. Aditi loved the way he stroked her head, gave her medicines and even fed her like a baby when the pain tore into her. Sometimes on a Saturday, mother and son would spend time chatting together.

'Rudra did you go to Bansdroni recently?'

'Yes mother. Everything is nearing completion. It needs only you to make the necessary decorations.' Rudra was lying . . .

'Decorations, my foot! I am not going to spend a single rupee on it except making furniture for your room.'

'Why?'

'Because as soon as we move into the house, I want you to get married.'

'No I am not going to get married now. I am just twenty-five, ma!'

'Rudra, my pet, twenty-five is a highly marriageable age. I hate old grooms. Besides, I want a daughter and grandchildren . . .'

'What else do you want ma?' He swallowed a sigh and continued, 'well let's first move and then we'll decide.'

'I think I should recover within a week, I am just impatient to go; aren't you?'

'Of course ma, but you must recover first.'

'Oh—of course I will!' Taking a deep breath she said, 'Rudra would you mind if I told you something?'

'No ma, why should I?'

'You know it's my wish to invite my folks to the house-warming party. My parents are still alive, I know. I will write them a letter, inviting them to our new house.' Rudra was visibly surprised. He had not seen his grand-parents. But he quickly got hold of himself.

'Sure ma.'

'But I know your father will be hurt. It will be for you to make him agree.' Rudra held his mother in his arms.

'Ma, I think you are mistaken, he will definitely fulfil your wishes.'

Rudra broached the subject to his father during dinner. 'Ma's health is deteriorating. Father, it's useless to defer going to the new house. Better stick to the date we had fixed earlier.'

'Son, do whatever she wants you to do. I have nothing to say.' He was tired.

'Father, there is one thing she requested me to ask you.'

'What is it?'

'Ma wants my grand-parents to come to the house-warming ceremony.'

'Of course they will be invited.'

'No-er-actually she wants 'her' parents to come and see the new house.' Robin was stupefied! For thirty years, his in-laws had not enquired whether their eldest daughter was alive or dead. They had sliced her off determinedly as a putrid segment of their lives, and now Aditi wants to invite them, to showcase their poverty!

'Out of the question!' He curtly shortened the conversation. Rudra knew that he had to bring his father to his senses. He responded, 'Father don't forget, it's ma's wish.'

Slinking inside the bedroom Robin looked at his wife intently. She was breathing heavily. In the faint glow of the night-lamp he could see the wisps of hair on her fair head. Under her eyes glistened the tears she shed a while ago. The mouth was taut in an attempt to suffocate the killing pain. He saw her tenuous body livened by the faint rising and falling of breaths, often punctuated by gasps and gurgles from her faded lips. Robin stood there rooted. He had only seen her writhing in pain and had run off from the room, scared and anguished. But that was different. Staring at him were the packed boxes, she had made ready with her failing strength, months before the day of departure. Robin felt a of sense of regret. She had done everything alone, jobs with which she was totally unaccustomed, for the only dream she had. After a few minutes he slid softly beside his wife and put his warm hand on her forehead. Aditi did not move. He stroked her hair, but she was in a sedated state. With a sigh he fell asleep beside her.

She woke up the next morning, refreshed. Rudra informed her that Robin had readily assented to her proposal of inviting her parents.

'Rudra, really! Rudra I just can't believe it! What did you tell him first?'

'I told you ma.'

'Do, tell me again, dear'.

'He said, "It will be so if your mother really wants it."'

'Really!'

'Ma, what's the big deal in that! Father always agrees to whatever you ask for.'

5th of May 1992 was the date fixed for the ceremony. The previous two days were hectic. The final packing, listing, sorting were done by Robin and Rudra who had taken leave from work. Aditi was restive but she was forced to recline on the bed and give orders to which she grudgingly agreed. She felt a wind in her bones, delightfully lifting up her spirits. The men bustled from one room to the other. Aditi fondly gazed at the old bed that both Robin and she had bought just after their marriage. She was to take it to the new house. She radiated an energy which caught up with the father and son. Robin was seen to smile after a long time.

'Look, I am walking now.' She strode proudly in front of him.

'You'll recover quickly when you go to the house.'

'Of course, I will! I already have.' She enquired about the preparations.

'The guests will all assemble there tomorrow. The priest has been called and the puja items are bought.'

'And flowers?' she asked.

'Yes of course. Plenty of flowers have been ordered as you wished.' Aditi was satisfied. Then with a slight frown she said, 'Robin I want to ask you something. Say you will answer me truthfully?'

'Er, what do you mean by "truthfully?" Have I ever lied to you, Diti?'

'No.'

'Well then, what is it!'

'Are you angry with me for inviting my parents?'

'Not at all! Why are you asking such questions?'

'Because they treated us so abominably!'

'No. I've forgotten the past.'

She took a deep breath and said, 'Thank you so much!'

Robin was sleeping like a log after the hard day's work. He was oblivious to the fact that Aditi frequently left the bed and vomited. Each retch left her drained. Still she did not wake up her husband and son.

'I'll be okay by tomorrow morning', she told herself.

At five-thirty in the morning Rudra discovered his mother lying on the veranda. She had dressed herself carefully in a red silk sari in which she was married, which Rudra had never seen her wear. On her forehead was described a red dot, she generally avoided wearing. Rudra had not seen her taking such pains in dressing up. He stared at his mother. His eyes grew moist. She looked so beautiful! Both father and son put her on the bed. A doctor was consulted. Gradually she recuperated and within an hour or so was fit enough to be moved to her new house. Aditi was extremely weak and was made to rest in her bedroom. She was restless and wanted to flit in and out of her rooms, but was restrained by her son and husband. She sat watching the puja in progress. After it was complete, she insisted on roaming the house which looked resplendent with the floral decorations. Drawing in the air into her lungs with renewed vigour, Aditi felt resurrected. She looked out, moved by the cluster of white on the dotted gray-bluish expanse of the sky. The lush green of the field awash with rain-water was a distant merge with the blue. She laughed and talked to her guests in abandon. Few could suspect that a couple of hours ago she had lain unconscious on the floor of her flat. Aditi had never looked so beautiful and her energy soared. Husband and son looked at her with amazement! It was a kind of transformation they had never thought would be possible for a woman who perhaps had only a few months to live. After sometime a limousine stopped near her house. Robin and Rudra stood outside the gate to welcome the invitees. A very old man and woman got down from the car, laden with gifts. They could not recognise the two men at the gate. It was Robin who went forward to receive them, forcefully discarding his inhibitions. He was extremely polite though formal and introduced his son to his grandparents who embraced Rudra with much fervour.

'Look he is like our Diti!' his granny remarked, holding on to him fiercely. Rudra felt her warmth slowly seeping into him, inundating him with a strange happiness. They took them to Aditi who was sitting inside her room. They entered. Aditi did not move. Her parents looked so old and vulnerable. She wanted to rush forward to greet them, but did not budge. Rudra and Robin were taken aback by her behaviour. Suren Chatterjee gauged her thoughts and spoke to her daughter.

'How old you look, Diti!' he exclaimed.

'I am nearing fifty,' was the reply.

Rudra made his grandparents comfortable by talking about various things and to hide his embarrassment. He failed to decipher his mother's attitude towards them. After all they were old and feeble. Robin stood in a corner of the room. A discomforting stillness pervaded there. Aditi's parents interpreted their daughter's silence as a grievance against them. Suren Chatterjee knew better. He requested Rudra to close the door.

'No!' screamed Aditi. There was an unseemly silence after which Chatterjee spoke.

'Diti, don't harbour any ill-feeling towards us my dear. We had done you a grievous wrong. Forgive us.'

'There is nothing to forgive,' she snapped.

She called Rudra to her and told him to make her parents sit where the guests were feasting. After finishing lunch they came back to placate their daughter. In Chatterjee's hands was a paper which he unrolled with a sense of glee and expectation.

'Diti,' he said 'I've brought you this.'

'What is it?' she asked, without touching it.

'This is a deed which I want to give you before we die. The house in Alipore where you grew up is yours now. I have bought a new smaller flat for us.'

'What about my younger sister?' she asked.

'Preeti is married and lives abroad. I have also given her a flat in Calcutta. She is possibly thinking of settling permanently in the UK.'

'So it is a measure to ease your conscience, isn't it?'

'I have told you that we have done you wrong.'

'And so you have come to gift me the house, in order to make it right? To bestow your pity on a beggar of a daughter whom you discarded thirty years before?' Rudra and Robin were extremely surprised and looked at each other in discomfiture.

'Insult me daughter! I deserve it. Only think that this gift is for Rudra, my grandchild.'

'Your grandchild! Hah! After thirty years! Listen; Rudra is not your grandchild and nor is he a beggar!' There was a telling silence.

'Diti, listen. Take this at least!'

Aditi's mother stepped out and opened a box full of jewellery. Seeing it, Aditi erupted with flaming rage.

'You want to bribe us with your possessions?' she questioned her mother.

'No Diti, it's not for you, if you don't wish to take it. But take it as a present for your to-be daughter-in-law.'

Aditi became more furious. 'How do you know that my daughter-in-law will need this shit?'

'Diti! Mother!' shouted Robin and Rudra.

'I don't need jewels. They are my jewels,' she pointed at her husband and son.

'Take away your gifts, each one of them. I don't need anything. I am happy as I am with my family. Rudra, put all the packets they have brought into the car. And be sure to show Mr. and Mrs. Chatterjee around this house before you help them out.'

REDEMPTION

Sunday morning. A knock at the door. He opened it, stunned, rooted to the spot. A few seconds passed before he could react.

'Let me in,' she said. There was hesitation on the other side. Looking at her face he acquiesced.

'Ok, come inside.'

The living room was the same. She sat down. The mother entered.

'You! How dare you come here!'

She responded coolly, 'I have come to talk to your son.'

'Talk to my son! After what you've done to him!'

'Done to him?'

'Yes, you finished him off. Ruined him forever!'

'Have *I* ruined him?'

'Yes after serving six months in jail he has been bailed out. There's no guarantee that he won't be imprisoned again. What kind of future do you think he has?'

'How dare you say this to me! To me! One who has been the victim of your son's lust! What sort of future do you think I have! A bed of roses? You say I ruined him! I, whom your son raped!'

He intervened.

'Mother, leave or stop shouting!'

'I won't. You know how I have spent my days without you;—lonely, miserable, with people saying such things . . . !'

'How funny; you are protecting the criminal just because he is your son and abusing the victim! One who has lost her dignity, her future, her life, for your son's insatiable lust!'

Again he came forward and took his mothers arm. 'Stop it ma, stop it I say!' Snubbed, she started wailing.

'You are the only one I live for. And you are scolding me for that nasty woman?'

'You have said this a thousand times after I came home; and now you are making my life a hell!'

'I have made your life a hell have I! How could you . . . ?' she cried aloud. He got up to steer her out of the room.

'No I won't go.'

'Then keep quiet.'

'Yes', he said, turning to the visitor, 'what do you want from me?'

'No, no, don't listen to what the bitch says.'

'Here, mind your language! How dare you talk to me like that!' she retaliated.

'Mother, I told you to stop!'

'I can't after what she has done to you!'

'Woman, get out and let me talk. I've been the one who has been ruined, not him! He has come back bailed out, enjoying himself with his friends. I know everything, every movement of your son. He has no right to enjoy himself when I am suffering! I who am innocent have been abandoned by friends and relatives and denied jobs!—I'm on the brink of death, not your son, remember that. Each day, each moment is a living hell for me. No money, no friends, no dignity. Roaming the streets like a dog; do you see justice in that? Do you think that I should be the sufferer, while he who desecrated me should be enjoying the warmth and luxury of a home?'

His face hardened. She looked at him, her eyes on fire!

'Don't listen to her, I'm warning you son. She's evil, she's brought evil into our lives and you are preparing to listen to her!'

'I won't have you talking in between.' The man got up, his teeth clenched. Putting his hands on his mother's shoulders he led her inside. Minutes ticked by. The girl waited. She guessed a consultation in progress. At last he entered the living room.

'What is the purpose of your visit?' the voice was grim.

'I have come with a proposition.'

'What proposition?' his face was hard and she could sense the raging fire of his sunken eyes on her.

'That you marry me.'

'What?' visibly startled, he looked at her.

'Look you've faced the consequences of your crime and I have become an outcast, through no fault of mine. Yet I am being treated worse than a whore. My family refused to take me in. My father gives me only a pittance—just to keep me alive! It doesn't even cover the house rent. I have to exist—somehow. I trusted you, you failed to keep it.'

'You want me to marry you and make amends for your—as you call it, "suffering"!'

'It is much more than that, I want my dignity back.'

'Oh! Dignity! How can I oblige you?'

'You are the only person who violated me. I had no relationship with anyone else. The onus lies on you to give me back my social standing by becoming your wife.' She was firm.

'But what about me? I haven't got a job and the case is on. There is every possibility that I may be jailed again. My future is equally bleak.'

'But it isn't worse than going back to jail again.'

'Yes, you're right. But how is it possible to avoid it?'

'That's the reason why I have come to talk to you.' She saw the quietly relaxed look on his face and continued,

'Look if you listen to what I say then we can both benefit by it.'

'Explain,' was his curt reply.

'If we both move court, saying that I have forgiven you and that you will marry me, then they may scrap the case altogether.'

He was deep in thought. She waited patiently for his reply. With a soft voice he said, 'I think we may try.'

But her voice was hard and flat. 'First we have to go to court. The sooner the better because it may take time.'

Both agreed to meet their respective lawyers. The court hearing their plea gave them three months for the final decision. Meanwhile they met. Two months elapsed. They conversed in restaurants and parks. The initial ice, the awkwardness, melted gradually. The blue-green played inside her. Then suddenly she experienced a red dissolve inundating her, the wetness running through her emaciated body. An indescribable surge of warmth! It was stunning! Bewildering! Did his gestures show a sign of contrition? She brushed away the thought. Observing him, did she discern a tinge of feeling? Bits and pieces of a room stood guards. Crimson. Only crimson. Covers, carpet, two gnarled barks with long branches. She shivered. Pushed to the floor and then—. The knees went weak. He bent to move a chair for her to sit, to comment on her looks and even proffer his handkerchief to wipe her moist forehead.

'Take this,' he would say almost tenderly.

'No thanks, I'm fine,' would be the blunt response.

'No you're not, you look terribly tired.'

'I'm okay, thank you.'

'You're thirsty. Shall I order a cold drink?'

'Ok if you wish!'

'I'm looking for a job. One of my friends has promised me.'

'I haven't any friends like yours.' Her voice was hard.

'I won't let you work.'

'Don't worry, we've already covered two months,' he continued,

'I am ashamed of what I had done to you! How could I do this to a friend! The more I see you the more guilty I feel! I know, it would be too much to ask, but will you forgive me?' She shuffled in her chair and kept silent. He tried to hold her hand.

'No,' she angrily, snatched it away.

'You hate me still! You don't believe me, do you? Not that I blame you. You are perfectly right in hating me. I don't deserve your forgiveness!' She kept quiet, unable to say anything. She tried to introspect. Did she feel an attachment to him? Then why look forward to these meetings? There was no answer. She had forgiven him. Yet there was a certain 'something' which stirred inside. Was it that 'something' she was scared of? Then why did she dream of the hibiscus rioting on her bed? Hibiscus. Plenty of them, each with a face of its own! Then she remembered. The park; she had seen them growing there. The answer dawned. She felt relieved.

There were further reassurances next week. 'I hope to get the job before we get married. You won't have to work.' She looked up surprised. He was leaning forward, his head was near hers. She responded by sitting rigid. Returning home she saw the hibiscus tree still red, dark red with the gleam of the setting sun. Slowly she became complacent. Within a month the case would be withdrawn. They would be married. People won't sneer, laugh or comment on her. Only a month, she thought with a sigh. The date of the marriage was fixed. He already had revealed his mother's acceptance of her. What could be better! She had pinned her hopes on the dismissal of the case. Life could be so inexplicable! Six months ago he had been her worst enemy and now she was waiting to become his wife! They had met so many times; was there a transformation in her? She wasn't sure. They began to meet oftener. He spoke like a man madly in love.

'After marriage we'll go for a honeymoon. What do you say to that?' She kept mum and raised her eye-brows. He was so garrulous!

'We'll try Puri. It would be within our means.'

'Why do we need a honeymoon? It's a marriage of convenience,' was the rejoinder.

'Don't hurt me like this!' his voice sounded intense, soft, burdened with love.

Looking at the table she responded pragmatically. 'It would be better if we shifted to another place where we are unknown, than spending money on trivial things.'

'Of course we'll shift from our filthy neighbourhood. But it will take time. First, the honeymoon. After marriage none will dare say anything! I'll do everything in my power to make amends for what I had done!' he clasped her hands, 'It's a matter of weeks!' He held her hands ardently.

She slowly released them and with an effort said, 'Will you really marry me?'

'How can you ask such a question! I can't go back on my word. And now it's not only a matter of keeping a promise.'

'Then what?'

'I love you.'

'Don't spin stories, I hate it!' Yet her heart pounded hard. She dared not believe what he said.

'I am not. I can't leave you now, not any more—I love you, passionately, sincerely.' He pressed her hand hard making her cry out in pain.

'I'm sorry. I had forgotten—I know you still hate me.'

'No,' she confessed, 'not now—not anymore.' The tendrils she had put to sleep; woke up with quivers of joy all over her body, making her unstable.

Weeks passed by, the friends returned. They would be the witnesses to the marriage. It would be a simple affair at the registration office. The case was dismissed. He now had a job through one of his many friends. Both of them decided that they wouldn't meet before the nuptials but would communicate verbally over the phone. They chatted often. Before the day of marriage he informed her that he would wait with his friends and his mother at eleven in the morning near the registration office. She rose early, bathed and examined herself in the mirror. She wore the silk saree he had given her as a present. It was blue with a crimson border. Walking to the place directed, she waited. It was already eleven o'clock. At eleven-thirty she went to a phone booth and rang him. A female voice answered. His mother. The girl said she was waiting.

'For whom?' asked the older lady.

'For your son,' she replied.

'My son? He left Calcutta last night.'

Crossing the park she saw the hibiscus tree still burning; the crimson flowers pushing down the leaves peeping through the grille. She caught hold of the turnstile to steady herself. Her head was reeling. She sat down on the pavement and saw the room, the scarlet curtains and the rosy carpet which sucked in all the red inside her.

THE MANSION

Nilima stared outside the window, fascinated by the storm that raced through the garden and lashed the trees with a vitriolic force of a monster on the rampage. Windows rattled, calendars flew off the walls, papers floated, utensils fell cluttering the floor, but she was unmoved. The spray spurted inside wetting her bed, her pillow, her body. Slowly, as the rage subsided, Nilima fell into a languor, the wetness somehow calming the turbulence inside her. She fell asleep on the moist armchair and dreamt again the same dream.

The huge mansion looked serenely beautiful, glinting in the last rays of the setting sun. Glossy pillars, black marbled steps, mosaic floors, carpeted halls, plush curtains, dazzling chandeliers—and Nili, as everyone called her, on her mother's knee in the garden. Then, the inevitable—the rusting, peeling, breaking,—dissolving into rubble—after which a phenomenal up thrust—an ugly blackened face-; diabolical—rising out of the netherworld—rising up, reaching for her. Frightened, Nili woke up and started to cry. Inside the still, decrepit wreck of a house, the sounds ran amok, hurtling through the dusty gloom of corridors, past the stairs to the garden. The rain had stopped. The afternoon drifted to purple and shadows of trees began to lengthen, describing sinister patterns on walls where darkness connived with yawning cavities of brick and sand.

Nili went to the terrace. She knew that the nightmares were nothing but the fall-out of her angst, eating into her existence. But somehow the explanation was not satisfactory. She leant over the parapet and looked down. Down below, was darkness and only darkness. The nearby houses were lit up and the sounds of evening pujas began. Nili sighed. Her once inchoate longing for a mate grew with age. She touched the coarse boundary that circumscribed her own life, with passionate intensity. She was forty. Her tortuous journey through the torrid zones alone, in the flush of her youth was perhaps a nemesis for an unrecognized sin, she thought.

Nili was not pretty. Not even pleasant to look at. She was born in Dacca before the partition of 1947. After independence, her father, a merchant, moved to Purulia in West Bengal. There he built a two-storeyed house and lived resplendently with his only child, wife and a retinue of servants. Nili lacked nothing. She went to a local school, passed the matric examination and stayed at home with her father, in wait for a prospective groom. Neighbouring families were too poor for the Sens to associate with. Rich youths with impressive backgrounds did not take a second look at her. And so Nili, companionless, aged. Surprisingly, in spite of her wealth, none made advances. After her father's death, she was left alone, trussed with the house. Yet Nili did not go to work, even though the expenses of maintaining the house did not become any cheaper. She thrived on her father's bank balance, but that too shrivelled with time. Getting rid of the servants, she fell to doing the household chores alone which of course helped to devour some bland hours of her life. Neighbours were few and friends or relatives fewer and far between. Standing on the terrace Nili wept, as the permeating smell of rain in the late evening air filled her nostrils.

One day, Vinay Sen, her father, came home carrying a packet. Eagerly unwrapping it, ten-year old Nili screamed with terror. He laughed, while her mother was visibly angry and shocked. Inside the wrapper was a horrid mask. The eyes somehow looked different, though menacing enough. They seemed to attract, mesmerize. Nili's father, captivated, bought it to amuse the little girl (who was getting pretty bored with the usual insipid fare of toys) from a roadside shop, whose owner was ready to sell it at half the price. The mask was made of paper mache, one of the many found in Purulia for which it is famous. Apart from the roguish eyes, the face sinuous with pockets of untidy beard looked as if the dirt of centuries' mischief lurked there. Nili's mother, aghast at the sight, shouted in disgust at her husband.

'Couldn't you find something better than this ghoulish face to gift your daughter?'

'Why, it's pretty interesting! Isn't it my pet? I guess, you are not silly to get frightened of a mere toy!'

'Why, what nonsense! Silly! She is only ten!'

With trembling hands Nili lifted the mask. She had to prove to everyone that she wasn't frightened. Not frightened at all!

From then on there grew Nili's uncanny affinity with the demonic visage. She carried it along with her through the huge mansion, talking, whispering, playing with it. When in a playful mood, she wore the mask to terrorize her mother, who hated the sight of it.

'Do you have to wear that horrid thing, do you?' she asked shuddering.

'Mummy, he's my friend. He talks to me you know; he's not bad, not bad at all. I like him.' Her mother's face whitened with the premonition of Nili's bizarre leanings. She severely reprimanded her daughter.

'Throw it out Nili! And immediately! I won't have you talking nonsense to it. Throw it out at once!'

'But ma, he hasn't done me any harm. I don't have friends. He is the only one I have. He speaks and plays with me. I love him mummy!'

Anima trembled with an inexplicable fear. She cursed her husband. Seizing the mask from Nili's hand, she threw it outside on the rubbish heap and gave her child a resounding slap on the cheek.

'That will put you in place. Toying with the devil! What a father—!' She gnashed her teeth and left the room. Nili cried, tears inundating her face. At night she dreamt of the mask and the rubbish dump. The eyes beckoned her. The bewitching eyes! She woke up in the wee hours of the morning and unnoticed went outside. The thing was still there. Throwing away all her inhibitions, she gingerly picked up the mask with her left hand and went to the courtyard. No one was around. On a nearby tree, crows made eerie noises. Nili opened the tap and let the water run on it. Then slowly, with the frill of her dress, she wiped it clean and went inside. Her room was still dark. A faint streak of morning light filtered through the slits between the curtains. The eyes were looking at her. With a little shiver she kissed the lips, climbed a chair and tossed the mask on top of a remote, dust-laden corner of a cupboard, not observable by anyone. But in her hurry to hide the forbidden object in semi-darkness, Nili failed to notice that her favourite plaything fell from the targeted place and was wedged between the rear boards of the furniture and the wall, from where it disappeared into oblivion. That day Anima collapsed, delirious with high fever and within a week she died.

The devastating loss in Nili's life was enough to erase even a vestige of memory of the mask. As she grew old, all her concerns centred on her father who was greatly altered after Anima's death. Her free hours were spent mostly roaming around the house and garden. Mr.Sen's efforts in securing a groom for his daughter did not mature. Prospective grooms scuttled away when they saw her and even the lure of the lucre failed to bring them back. Gradually she gave up being concerned about her marital prospects. But Mr. Sen was desperate to get her settled. To Nili's utter exasperation, unemployed, middle-aged men were wooed with the intention of getting a stay-in husband for her.

'Father, what do you really want? Marry me to any baggage and drown me? Or do you want me to walk out of this house?' Her father couldn't utter a word. Relatives came in droves, trying to act as intermediaries between father and daughter. Nili drove them out of the house. She wanted to be alone. The huge mansion was intoxicating. She flitted from room to room talking to herself. It was as if the house waited for communication with her. Her bedroom in the southern corner of the building was her favourite. She spent long hours minutely observing a little crack on the rear wall near the cupboard. The servants laughed, thinking that her psychic peregrinations were only for a long-lost love.

Mr. Sen died suddenly of a stroke when Nili was just forty. Suddenly there was a hiatus between Nili's pragmatic self and with the other, who entertained her, accompanied her throughout the house and perambulated through her wildest fantasies. Yet certain practical considerations had to be taken into account. She had to survive and survive alone. The house weaved a spell around her. Getting rid of the servants, she fell to working by herself; cleaning, dusting, washing. The world outside, though meaningless now to her, had to be confronted. Monthly visits to the bank, settling accounts, paying dues, weekly shopping, continued. These necessities tapered from the regular to the frequent and gradually to the occasional. Neighbours saw her walking alone to the market. Whispers buzzed in the air.

'Wonder how she lives alone, in that great house!'

'She's crazy, you know, that's why. Look, there she goes talking to herself—'

'Surprising, she isn't scared living alone like this!'

'None goes near that old house after dark!'

'Her eyes, so strange, aren't they?'

Nili imbibed the scent of disapproval in the air and recoiled in disgust. How she hated those common women! It was revolting to think that she had once entertained the thought of renting the house! She went indoors, tears welling up in her eyes, seeing the fading colours of her beautiful house, the riot of creepers in the corners and the run—on cracks on the walls; exposing its lacerated veins. It was beyond her means to restore it. The garden, no matter how much she slaved, wouldn't thrive. It was full of ugly clumps of grasses. The trees, most of which stood like leafless skeletons, mocked her. At night, she retired to her own little room and stared vacantly for hours at the peeling plasters and the crack that travelled aimlessly along the wall of her room. Sometimes she fell asleep while ruminating and dreamt the same dream.

Nili's self-imposed isolation distanced her neighbours so much that few ever came to enquire after her. The gradual transmutation of a cheerful young girl to a surly old woman who kept to herself, muttering gibberish, only raised speculations about her sanity. Deliberately, queries of concerned neighbours were made redundant by hints of interference. Offers of help were sternly rejected. She grew old, oblivious to the demands of her body. In the mirror Nili saw wrinkles; saw criss-crossing cracks on the walls of her room—her tanned skin standing out against the darkened paint that chronicled the wasted years of her youth. Looking at herself she cried. A burst of uncontrolled, heart-wrenching sobs shook her. The sounds pierced through the mansion and reverberated through the corridors and halls. The house seemed sentient to Nili. She fell on the bed and cried herself to sleep.

Sunday was the only day when Nili ventured outside, ambling along with a shopping bag to the market. Haggling was hateful to her. She paid without a word, even though she felt she was cheated. Nili was a prized customer who communicated in monosyllables. Eager eyes played on her back and whispers floated along with the smell of scaled fish, to which she never gave attention. She recoiled at the touch of the shopkeepers on her fingers, when she paid them. Taking out her handkerchief she vigorously rubbed off the faintest trace of sensation, as if she was erasing the memory of an unavoidable crime. People tore her apart when she left.

'Stuck-up bitch, that woman. Too high and mighty!'

'Good customer though. Look at some of these women haggling, as if their whole life depended on a piece of coin!'

'But too proud! Treats us like dirt!'

'Poor thing! Lost her mother when she was a child. Had to run a family and look after an invalid father.'

'But too plain for anyone to marry her. How old she looks! How she lives alone in that old house I wonder!'

'I've heard she practices witchcraft. People are scared to go near the house after dark!'

'Haven't you anything better to do than accusing an old woman for nothing just because she keeps to herself!'

'Oh what do you have here! A big fan of hers! Had a secret rendezvous, I bet!'

'Shut up you bastards! Tearing up a lady to pieces just because she doesn't go chattering with you! Are you human beings?'

Nili didn't know that there were one or two dissenting voices amongst the scandalmongers in the market place who spoke up for her. Not that she cared the least. Instead she stared fascinated at a crack that extended from one end of the ceiling of her room to another.

One day, a letter arrived. It was from a classmate, who was once very attached to Nili. Dipa had often been in her house as a child, where she was always welcome. At sixteen, she was married and soon left for the UK, where her husband worked. After Dipa left Purulia, there wasn't any communication between the two. The letter reminded Nili of her childhood and her heart was swept with indefinable sensations. Dipa and her husband Deb were leaving UK for good and were to settle permanently in their ancestral home in Calcutta where the latter had found a job. Since there was a lot of time on their hands, Dipa suggested that they visit Purulia where she once lived. Her parents were dead and the house, sold out. She longed to see her childhood friend before her husband settled down in Calcutta. Nili wrote promptly, inviting them to her house. They were to spend at least a fortnight with her. A sudden elation gripped her, and as the day of arrival drew near, she briskly started working, to put the house in order.

One morning just before the day of Dipa's arrival, she discovered the mask from the rear depths of the cupboard. It was almost unrecognisable, bruised by the oblivious dust of decades. A strange metamorphosis occurred when she cleaned it and the diabolical visage was gradually resurrected. A certain joy, a phenomenal up thrust of the "other"; the irresistible, unfathomable and unidentifiable 'something' gripped her psychic passage. She put the mask on top of the cupboard, from where she could see it. The eyes,-the mesmeric eyes held her captive.

The next day, Dipa and Deb arrived. The women hugged each other ardently. Even after forty, Dipa was still very attractive, and with Deb by her side, they looked tailor-made for each other. They brought gifts for Nili which warmed her heart. The couple was childless. Living abroad for many years they often forgot to maintain the rural proprieties, and hugged and kissed each other in front of Nili. Nili avoided those moments with an excuse. She served delicious meals with her meagre resources. They gossiped, the threesome, about their own lives, specially the ladies; raking up the cinders of half-forgotten childhood days. Nili refused household help and offers of shopping (which became almost regular) and did everything to please her friend and her husband. Days elapsed. The couple was overwhelmed by Nili's hospitality.

Every night they retired to the east wing of the house, which was mammoth strong. A bedroom at the far end was made ready for them. Nili didn't feel tired even after the whole day's labour. Staring at the mask gave her strength and unmentionable sensations. With a candle she moved along, drawing strange shadows on the corridor walls which led to Dipa's bedroom. There were sounds that told stories of love and desire. Nili's eyes grew fierce, nostrils twitched and her body became tense. She went back to her room and looked at the mask. There was fire and water inside her. Then determinedly she said to herself,

'No. No. Never.'

In the morning she went to the market. Her friend was angry.

'Nili, why don't you let us go for shopping?'

'You really needn't bother about it,' was the reply. It was her house and she was the mistress!

'Then we must go back to Calcutta tomorrow.'

'You certainly shall not. I forbid it.' There was something singular in Nili's voice which prevented Dipa from being importunate.

'She must have her own reasons,' she surmised. There was a tinge of pity for her frail, helpless, old playmate.

Meanwhile the regular shopping ventures of the surly old woman created ripples in the market. It was a rickshaw-puller who had brought the visitors to the huge mansion who unveiled the secret of Nili's regular shop-hopping. The shop-keepers were exhilarated!

'Let her have plenty of visitors.'

'Yes it's the time to make some money.'

They laughed behind her back but behaved with her deferentially. None of them dared to make queries to appease their gut-rumbling curiosity. Nor did anyone go and take a look at the new inmates of the house. They were too intimidated by her and let her alone with them.

One day Deb and Dipa went for a tour of Purulia. They rented a rickshaw and left. Nili was alone in her room. Automatically, her eyes roved and halted on the top of the cupboard. She sat there for a few minutes as if in a trance—immobile. Then with a start, she stood up in a state of daze and went to the shed. Taking a hammer and a big nail she moved along like a screwed-up automaton wired for a gun toting feat. Half an hour later on Dipa's bedroom door was discernible a hole through which the whole room could be viewed. Satisfied, she went back to her room and stared at the crack on the ceiling with a strange anticipation.

Nili greeted her friends with a huge smile so rare for her, when they returned. Dipa was surprised to see the bony almost ugly face light up with delight. Afternoon was quietly turning to purple, when the couple retired to rest. The door closed. Inside their bedroom was a hide-and-seek of pink and yellow. Nili locked her eyes inside the gaping circle she made. Her face stiffened, hands trembled, knees quaked, but she looked on and on, sucking in the scene, the hair on her skeletal hands bristling with a vicarious sensation. At last it was over and the bedroom melted into dark.

It was a sultry day. The heat was oppressive. Streets were bare and a few people who could not avoid going outside were seen hurrying fast to get indoors before the heat became unbearable. Shops were partially closed or awnings spread out to ward off the melting heat. Soon it swirled around the town, a prelude to the coming storm. Around three in the afternoon the sultriness increased and the air became still and suffocating. Sensing the lull to be that of the usual nor'wester, people did not take chances and headed home as fast as they could.

Anticipating a drenched evening, Nili went to the kitchen to prepare khichuri (a delicacy savoured specially during rainy days) which was Dipa's favourite dish. She volunteered to help Nili but was sent back to her husband. Distressed, Dipa complained, 'Nili why do you send me away when we have come specially to spend time with you?'

'No darling, your husband may feel left out.'

'Who bothers? I want to talk to you!'

'Yes dear, of course. I'll come as soon as I've finished with the chicken.'

'Who told you to take such pains for us?'

'It's my pleasure. I live alone and after so many years I have found my only friend for whom it's a delight to cook.'

Dipa stopped arguing. 'Ok, but please hurry!' she left; her eyes moist, touched by the affection of her friend.

By eight-thirty, a tempest was brewing; the rumble extending from the outskirts to the heart of the town itself. It swept through within five minutes, leaving death and destruction in its wake. Trees were uprooted with electrifying speed, roofs toppled by the unbridled rage of the whirling wind that scattered dust and grime along its way. Meanwhile Nili dined with her friends. It was an excellent dinner. The conversation turned nostalgic once again. But the couple felt unusually sleepy that night, and retired early. They too were terrified by the menacing thrust of the storm and requested Nili to come to the eastern wing of the house where there was a bedroom, since the southern part of the mansion was almost dilapidated. But no amount of logic or reason could deter her from retiring to her own chamber. Dipa and Deb terribly sleepy, after scouring the town the whole day, stopped arguing and went to bed. The rampage of wind and water went on unabated throughout the night. Terror ran inside houses of the people who apprehended insuperable losses of life and property. The storm was not the usual nor'wester that people welcomed during summer. Its apparently innocuous start contradicted the outcome that transformed the lives of the unsuspecting villagers.

Then an unexpectedly bright day signalled the end of the terrifying nightmare, unveiling the spectacle of ruin and death. Frightened, dejected crowds gathered here and there to gauge the comprehensiveness of the carnage and estimate the losses incurred by it.

It was about eleven-o'clock in the morning when a boy ran to the market place where the villagers had gathered, to discuss the night's disaster. Breathless and pale he screamed at the startled group.

'The house, the huge house near the rice field has collapsed!'

'What?'

'I went there and saw it myself!'

'Don't play pranks boy, how can such a big house collapse?'

'May be he's right. The house was dilapidated alright.'

'Perhaps—but the woman!'

'The woman! The woman!' they cried in unison.

The southern wing of the house had crumbled. The rest of the mansion stood tall, a mute witness to the wreck surrounding it. The rubble was extensive. The bedrooms had caved in. On a cluster of wooden planks amidst the brick heap, was where they found her body. There was no sign of wound anywhere. She lay as if in a sleep.

'Poor thing,' said the villagers.

The eastern side of the house was massive and rooted to the ground. The men combed that part which strongly resisted the blast. A bedroom at the far end of the corridor was untouched. The door was locked from the inside. They broke in. A couple lay on the bed. There was a faint stench. The villagers held their noses and went inside. Stone-dead. At least twelve to fifteen hours ago, they guessed. Suddenly a boy screamed. On the dressing table was a mask with a smile on its lips.

THE KNOT

Apolyclinic in Calcutta. A man of about thirty-five rushed to the desk of the appointment coordinator. As the latter saw him, his face contorted with anger.

'How many times have I told you that Dr. Sengupta will not be free till next month! There isn't any place where I can insert your wife's name. Please try to understand that. I can give you an appointment for the first available date of the next month. That will be the earliest.'

'Look I've already told you that my wife is extremely ill. She will not survive if I do not consult him immediately!'

'Mr. Das, I am helpless. Why not consult another doctor? There are so many!'

'I insist she be treated by him, because he's the best for her.'

'Then I am very sorry, I can't oblige you,' replied the skull faced, toady-eyed man; adjusting his too big horn-rimmed glasses.

'You will have to, it is serious.'

'Mr. Das, there are many other seriously ill patients, waiting just for Dr. Sengupta for months!'

'I don't care. My wife is dying, you must do something! It's an emergency!'

'My hands are tied, I'm sorry!'

The polyclinic was full of patients. Mr. Das waited for a minute and then disappeared. The man at the desk uttered a sigh of relief. His sunken cheeks inflated slightly and the roach-feelers like moustache relaxed. Unfortunately, his relief was temporary. The roach-feelers were up again. Das popped up the next day, when the clinic was chock-a-block with patients. His jaws were set, his eyes were on fire. Seeing him again, the roach became apprehensive. The feelers were steely-taut with tension. Beads of perspiration dotted his forehead. He mentally readied himself for a confrontation. To his surprise the man instead of going up to him, waited at the door. It took a few minutes for the egg-headed roach to understand his motive. A patient was still inside Dr. Sengupta's chamber. But it was too late. The roach jumped from his seat when Mr. Das rushed in as soon as the visiting patient got out. There was a terrible furore. Dr.Sandip Sengupta lost his cool and yelled at him for being unable to restrain Mr. Ashok Das.

'What are you doing Mr. Roy? If you have no control over the patients, why sit and take appointments?'

Mr. Roy shrivelled like a leaf on fire. Knees quaking he croaked, clutching his pants desperately. He badly needed to pee and now his trousers were slipping off! 'Sir, er, this man, Mr. Das has been pestering me to get—an appointment for his wife. He came yesterday; I refused him saying you were filled up for this month. He didn't listen and entered by force—what can I do sir?'

Meanwhile Mr.Das was inside the chamber. Dr.Sengupta, impatient to avoid more trouble looked at the distraught stranger. He had a bevy of patients waiting and was already tired after a number of operations. With a resigned voice he questioned Mr. Das.

'Don't you know that it's wrong to deprive other people who had come before you; people who have been waiting for months for a visit?'

'I know sir. I apologise for that. But there was no other option for me. My wife is dying. She won't survive this month if you don't treat her!'

'What were you doing all this time?'

'She suppressed everything from me till it was too late!'

'What is her problem?' His voice seemed resigned with exhaustion.

Mr. Das elaborated on the nature of the disease and insisted that she be treated by Dr. Sengupta only. He had heard that he was an expert in his wife's case. After hearing Mr. Das's description, he looked serious and suggested immediate treatment. Dr. Sengupta thought for a minute and asked Mr. Das to bring his wife the next day as a special case.

'What's her name?' he queried.

'Sulagna Das.'

'OK, bring her tomorrow at seven p.m. I'll enter her name in the register.' Thanking the doctor profusely, Mr.Das left, reassured.

The next day a very fair and pretty but frail looking lady in her early thirtics was helped inside Dr. Sengupta's chamber by her husband. He was not there. Exhausted by the short walk, she reclined on a chair.

Sulagna wore a very cheap, printed cotton sari and sandals. But on her face was a polish of dignity and reserve which was noticeable.

Minutes passed by like days. The patient was in pain but the doctor was absent. At last the door opened. He entered and kept his bag on the table with his back turned to them and addressed her casually, 'Yes what's your problem?' As she ventured to answer, he turned, his eyes riveted on her. There was a gasp of astonishment on both sides.

'Sulagna, you? How come . . . . ?' he couldn't continue any longer.

She was shaken, 'Why, I didn't know . . .'

Ashok Das sat staring at them.

Trembling inside, she sensed the awkwardness of the situation and introduced the doctor to her husband, 'Dr. Sengupta was our neighbour when I was at my father's.'

'Oh! What a pleasant surprise,' he responded with a smile.

'It's more than eight years since we met!' The doctor was ecstatic! He was forgetting the time. Sulagna, mud-footed, veered the recollections, to remind him of her ailment, in a dry matter-of-fact tone. As the doctor listened to her, he grew more and more concerned. His physical examination was seriously formal, yet she still felt the sensations his touches sent through her as of old. He suggested that she immediately get admitted to a nursing home of his preference. An operation had to be done and it was complicated. There was no other option. He continued, 'Either choose to be operated or die a painful death.' He was serious.

'I can't die, I have a family,' she responded.

'Then do what I tell you and leave the rest to me.'

The very next day Sulagna was admitted to Getwell. It was a modest care-centre with modern amenities. The couple realised that even the expenses of this ordinary nursing home would be too much of an economic strain for them. Ashok's income as a clerk in a private firm and the little savings they had would not suffice to cover the cost, not to mention the post-operative expenditure. There was no other alternative but to borrow.

Sulagna's life was at stake. To Ashok that was the most important thing. Sitting on the bed of the nursing home she thought of the various ways possible to curtail the family expenditure. When Dr. Sengupta visited her, he saw a worried expression on her face. He put it down as anxiety and fear of the next day's ordeal. He excused the nurse to be alone with her.

'Why are you so glum? Scared?' he smiled.

'It's nothing of the sort.' After a while she asked, 'Dr. Sengupta, can you furnish me with a rough estimate of the expenses that this operation will incur?' She was blunt.

'It's nothing to be worried about. Bare minimum.'

'I'm not a fool. Tell me. I'll have to take some measures, to get the money.'

'What, beg, borrow or steal?' he laughed.

'I'm serious, Dr. Sengupta.'

'Sulagna, don't call me Dr. Sengupta. You hurt me.'

'You are Dr. Sengupta aren't you?'

'Why on earth do you dislike me so much?'

'Don't you realise that discussing the past will be of no use? Isn't it better that we relate to each other as only a doctor and a patient?'

'You are cruel Sulagna!'

'I am Mrs. Das now, Dr. Sengupta.' The voice was firm.

'Ok, ok I know. Take rest. You need the strength to cope up with tomorrow's operation!' He called the nurse back and ordered her to continue with the pre-operative preparations and left. Sulagna watched him going out of the room. He was still so handsome, with the same rich voice, the same intent expression! Drops of tears made their way down her cheeks. No matter how much she tried she couldn't bridle the emotion that haunted her still.

The operation was a success. It lasted for four hours and was complicated. But he got through it and the patient was responding well to the treatment. When she was convalescing in the nursing home, he visited her. The nurse retired after showing the medical chart. He was satisfied.

'Well how are you feeling now, Sulagna?'

'Dr. Sengupta, I'm so grateful! You've given me a new life—not to me only, my family too.'

'Don't talk to me about gratitude. I would have done anything to save you. Don't talk like a patient to me.'

'Do you realise doctor that I am married and extremely attached to my family! I shall be obliged if you talked to me as you would to a patient.'

'I can't when I see you. After I came back from the UK, I searched for you everywhere. At your father's, friends'—everywhere. You were lost. I had given up hope. And now when I have found you, after eight years, you want me to act doctor! How strange!'

Sulagna kept quiet. The resistance inside was cracking up. When he left, she debated within herself. How could she still love him after what had happened! Besides, she was attached to Ashok deeply! Was there anything wrong in her mindset? Was it possible to love two people at the same time? Guilt-ridden, she remonstrated with herself. Did she only feel gratitude towards Ashok? Was her heart with Sandip all these years! Unfaithful then, she was to her husband! Shuddering at the thought, Sulagna ventured to mentally resurface Ashok's unstinted devotion to her. He was her life! Then there was Tutun, her son! This thought unnerved her! Unfettered, unabashed droplets fell, moistening the arid cheeks. The attendant entering the cabin was about to rush to the doctor, when she wiped her eyes and prevented her from doing so.

'I'm okay.'

'But you're crying in pain madam!'

'It's nothing. Please let me alone.'

Sulagna recovered quickly. She was about to be released from the nursing home. Ashok went to pay the bills which to his astonishment were unexpectedly paltry. Did Dr. Sengupta perform this miracle? If so, they would have to pay him back! Unlikely that he would take the money. Ashok caught up with the doctor who was on his way to visit a patient.

'I'll meet you in Mrs. Das' cabin.'

'Ok sir.'

Ashok mentioned the meagre sum he had to pay, to his wife. To his surprise she was not amazed.

'He knew me very well, that's why,' was what she replied.

When Dr. Sandip Sengupta came to Sulagna's cabin for the final check-up, Ashok introduced the subject. The doctor seemed to be surprised too, or so it appeared. Asked whether it was his beneficence or not, he answered in the negative. Then hurriedly he started examining the patient as if he wanted to discard the redundant topic. Satisfied with her physical condition, he suggested that he come to their house for weekly checkups. Sulagna fought to keep her cool, while Ashok was unable to believe his good luck and effervesced with gratitude like fizz in a bottle. He gave him his address saying,

'Doctor I owe my wife's life to you, and now, instead of our visiting you, you have undertaken the duty of visiting her, in spite of your busy schedule! How can I thank you!'

'There is no need to thank me!' He patted Ashok's shoulder with amicable condescension. 'She was once my neighbour. It will be my pleasure to come and chat with you on Sundays. Just forget the duty factor.'

She looked at him. There was that old darkish-deep look in his jet-black eyes, that burgeoned thrills all over her and escaped Ashok's eyes. She silently tided over them.

The Sundays seemed to come inordinately late for the doctor. By some inexplicable trick of fate he had at last discovered the girl he had always loved. It was only for her that he deliberately remained single, though she was coerced, he surmised, to get married. There was a child but he would not be a problem if there was a divorce. He would bring him up as his own son and sacrifice the need for his own, to make Sulagna happy. He could not bear to see her in such a dismal, pecuniary condition. It broke his heart. He did not reveal that nearly all the bills of Getwell were paid by him. He hungered to gift Sulagna a lavish life-style. She deserved it. He had enough money for that! It had to be! Sandip rolled over the reminiscing grasslands and hankered after the incandescent skyline, he thought was within his reach.

Ashok wasn't the least suspicious about the prior relationship of Sulagna and Sandip. Without mentioning any name she had confided everything in him even before their marriage. He had an implicit faith in her love and devotion which generated a sense of peace and happiness in his heart. After their marriage, Sulagna, guilt-ridden, often tried to gauge his feelings towards her.

'I know you pity me Ashok!'

'What makes you think that?'

'Everyone has left me, my parents, relatives, and friends. You only have been my saviour!'

'Sulagna, you know that I love you. Why do you keep asking such silly questions?'

'Because, everyone, even your parents have abandoned you because of me! I have caused so much pain to them!'

'I tried to make amends by offering to stay by their side. They refused. Besides they have other sons to look after them! They are fine!'

'But you miss your parents—only for me!'

'Yes I do. But there's no other alternative. I can't go to a place where my wife will be disrespected!'

'It's my fault. If only I could control myself that day!'

'Why do you brood about the past? Have I not accepted everything?'

'Yes; but with so much to lose!'

Ashok did not reply but drew his wife closer to him. 'I don't want to hear these things anymore, do you understand?'

He hugged her and they made love.

Sulagna wondered why after nearly eight years, the pain which she thought was scrubbed off; reappeared, when she saw Sandip. After what he had done to her—deserting her during a crisis—but she had to admit that it was not entirely his fault. If he had known her condition—then, perhaps—she was too angry and dejected—reminiscences would come. It was strange, the love she thought was only a tombstone—to be so quickly bulldozed; the spectre resurrected by a glance, by a word,—Oh! God, how could she get rid of the dilemma—! Then again, he had searched for her all these years—remained a bachelor, then saved her life, the life she needed for her husband and son! Foam-floating emotions, she thought. So evanescent. But no. She couldn't forget the day they had made love—he didn't know the rest. Deliberately he was kept in the dark. The terrible, engulfing passion she could not resist—will she tell him? Her husband did not know it was Sandip—! Sulagna shuddered to think of the consequences.

One Sunday Ashok was away from the house. Sandip arrived as usual. He had succeeded in befriending Tutun, whom he showered with toys and chocolates. Sulagna reprimanded,

'You are spoiling him doctor!'

'It does no harm to spoil children sometimes.'

'Please don't say this. We can't afford all these expensive things that you give him. You are raising his expectations!'

'You are too harsh on me, Sulagna.'

She kept quiet. No use arguing. Looking down on the floor she steeled herself. She did not observe that he came and sat beside her. He tried to take her hand in his. She drew it away.

'I think you should stop visiting me every Sunday. I'm fine now.'

'Do you think I come to check your health only?' he smiled.

'You do not need to elaborate.' Her voice was grim.

'Sulagna, you don't understand that I love you still!'

'Please, I am another man's wife.'

'I know. Why did you ever go and marry him? What does he have? No money, no looks, nothing!'

'Please be decent enough not to disparage my husband before me! I have not given you leave to do that!'

'Don't be so angry. Ok, I'm sorry. But why did you marry? Didn't you have any faith in me? I'm still waiting for you!'

'You left me when I needed you most,' she curtly responded.

'But you know I had to make a career! How could I have given up the opportunity to go abroad to get a degree! Sulagna you are unreasonable!'

'Me, unreasonable? Did you ever stop and think of the consequences of the night we made love?'

'What do you mean?'

'Even after two months of the incident, did you inquire about my condition?'

'I don't understand!' Then after a brief silence he said, 'what!'

'You never tried to, but left for the UK.' Sulagna interrupted. Sandip was excited and almost shouted with irritation.

'Sulagna, will you explain? Please?'

'I was pregnant when you left me.'

'Then why didn't you tell me? Oh! God!'

'You wouldn't have listened to me, you were career-crazy. Drunk with ambition. You would have told me to abort it.'

'You are wrong, absolutely wrong! You didn't even intimate me in the letters abroad! I would have come and married you and taken you back with me!'

'It's easy to say these things now when you are wallowing in wealth and luxury! Your letters never spoke of your concern for me! They sounded only of your rising careeristic endeavours! I was mortified! Heartbroken. I buried my love and resolved to have the baby, severing all contacts with you. Those were my darkest days. My parents, discovering my condition, drove me out. But I refused to divulge your name to anyone because the love we made was precious to me and I did not want it to be tarnished in any way. No one was beside me. Not even my friends. My world collapsed! It was an abysmal darkness—there was no hope. Everyone treated me as if I were a leper. Shall I have to expatiate more on the plight of an unmarried pregnant girl! It was at this juncture that Ashok came to my life, accepted me as I was; who never for once, asked me the name of the man, and married me unconditionally. He gave me back what I had lost. He is my light, my world, my life. He left his parents because of me, he nursed me when I was in labour! He loves me, heart and soul! Who are you now? A doctor, and I, a patient, that's all. It's all over Sandip. I love my family! Yes you saved my life, I'm grateful to you for that!' her voice quivered. She was breathless.

Minutes ticked by. The anguish tore him apart. Then suddenly, Sandip's eyes lit up.

'Then Tutun? He is my boy! I have a right over him!'

'No, he is Ashok's child.'

'But what happened to my baby?'

'He was still-born.'—Then after a fraction of a second she continued, 'Please do not visit us again.'

When Sandip left, Sulagna burst into tearing floods! She fell on the bed and cried, 'I lied to you Sandip. Tutun is your son. Our son.'

THE RETURN

The rusty gate creaked open. One by one the few remaining neighbours entered the huge courtyard. Set against the blackened ruin of the Chowdhury mansion, two boys clung to each other and wept. Sachin slowly freed himself from Jamal and walked towards the gate. The carriage was waiting. Bidding farewell to the onlookers, he gave the keys to Jamal's father Hassan and entered the vehicle. A dark shadow rested on the courtyard. The small crowd emptied, as Hassan locked the gate for the last time in his life.

Sachin's forebears were residing for many generations in Begumpur in undivided Bengal. Rathindra his grandfather, was a zamindar, the owner of a huge landed property. But when his son Manindra inherited the estate he found to his dismay that his father's profligacy had depleted the family fortune by more than half. Besides this, encroachments on the land by people of questionable repute had left the estate shrivelled and riddled with many problems. Manindra dared not use his power to evict those people who had permanently settled on the greater parts of the land he owned. These men had strong discriminatory religious views. Another reason for his passivity was that as early as 1930, communal riots were not uncommon. Manindra was a victim of circumstances on which he had no control. The Chowdhury estate had shrunk to a few cottahs with a few devoted tenants when Sachin was born.

Hassan's father Harun was one of the few loyal subjects who had once savoured Rathindra Chowdhury's magnanimity. He was the overseer of the estate and in his time wallowed in his landlord's munificence. When his son took up his father's job, things were not the same. There was almost no land that needed management. He had no other option but to become the caretaker of the Chowdhury mansion. Hassan and his family lived within the precincts of the estate in a small two roomed house where Jamal was born. In spite of the disparity in socio-economic standing, Manindra did not allow that to come in the way of attachment between the two families who were very closely connected to each other for generations. He sponsored Jamal's education; and Sachin, two years older than his friend, was always by his side. The intensity of their friendship created an invulnerable bond. By nature Sachin was an introvert and Jamal, an incorrigible prankster; who often invited complaints from the neighbours, robbed of their mangoes and bananas from their gardens. Often scared of his father's thrashings he would appeal to Sachin for succour. The older boy became his saviour:

'Don't worry Jamu. I'll take the blame.'

'But they won't believe you, they won't!'

'If I take the blame none will contradict me.'

'I've heard Badri will bring others along to complain against me to uncle Mani. He has seen me.'

'Let's see what we can do.'

The next day the villagers arrived with complaints against Jamal's savage exploits. Manindra became serious.

'Is it true Jamal?' Sachin stepped out promptly.

'I have done it father, not Jamu.'

'No, no, it's Jamal!' there was a crescendo of horrified voices.

'We saw him with our own eyes!' they cried.

'No I did it.' Sachin was firm. Manindra raised his stick to silence the furore.

'Open your shirt!' he ordered sternly. Sachin complied and started undoing his buttons. There was a hush of stupefaction. Then Hassan unable to restrain himself cried out:

'Sir, it's Jamal my son and no one else!' Manindra, heedless, raised his stick. Suddenly bursting into sobs Jamal veered round the wielded weapon and fell on Sachin's shoulder, encircling him in order to receive the raging cane on his back. Manindra was moved beyond words and so were the villagers, to witness the spectacle. The matter ended with the landlord's assurance of compensation to the complainants.

Jamal and Sachin spent their childhood within the circumscribed world of their estate, impervious to the political turmoil that troubled the outside world. But it was not for long. After his mother Suhashini's death, Sachin drifted along like a rudderless vessel, battered by a monstrous hurricane. It was Jamal who steered hard to anchor him, by his constant vigilance. Sachin, vulnerable in the abysmal darkness found solace in

Jamal. His mother Sabina looked after the boy and the two friends came closer to each other as never before. The turbulence in the country was far from over. The whirlwind of national politics that sucked India in, did not leave the Chowdhurys unscathed. In 1947, the formation of East and West Pakistan and India's independence were the two divergent fall outs of the struggle for freedom under British supremacy. It had left India emancipated but trussed with several problems of great magnitude. The partition had already ruptured the nerve centre of all positive values of Bengali life. The interpenetrating socio-cultural and religious co-existence was vandalised. Riots broke out in East-Pakistan conducive to the exodus of many Hindus who migrated to India.

By 1950, Begumpur (which became a part of East-Pakistan) was also reeling under the negative vibrations that rocked the country. The Chowdhurys noticed that a few of their Muslim neighbours were behaving unnaturally with them. Manindra was not keeping well after his wife's death and at a very young age Sachin was at the helm of the estate, scarred with grievous problems. The name East-Pakistan had an unsteadying effect on Sachin and Manindra. They would become jittery at the mere mention of riots. Jamal wondered why Sachin sometimes looked at him questioningly. In January 1950, there were reports that armed pro-Pakistani fanatics had arrived in Begumpur to attack the Chowdhury mansion.

The news spread like forest-fire and soon reached Manindra's ears. One or two Hindu neighbours that lived near the estate vanished overnight. So did the servants and relatives of Manindra. He stubbornly refused to leave his ancestral home and urged his son to quit the mansion with his cousins. Sachin did not budge. At 1 a.m. in the night, a stranger, his face covered with a shawl, appeared in his room. Before Sachin could utter a word he took out a gamchha (towel) and deftly tied his mouth by pinning him down on the bed with his knees. Sachin was hauled out of the room and taken outside in the dark.

Within half-an-hour the whole mansion was looted and set ablaze. Still insatiable, the crowd went berserk, and shouting at the top of their voices arrived at Jamal's house. Trembling violently, Hassan opened the door. Familiar faces. Very familiar. Armed, blood-stained, carrying torches. Visages on which gleamed the mad hunger for blood. One of them held a knife at Hassan's throat and made way for others to enter. In the outer room they found Jamal. Hitting him hard with the hilt of a sword they asked for Sachin.

'Where is your friend?'

'I don't know.'

'You don't know you bastard!' They pulled him off the bed and searched under it. Jamal was beaten and kicked relentlessly till blood oozed from his mouth.

'Licking Hindu feet, you dog! We'll crush the life out of you if you don't tell us where he is!' He felt his hand being twisted. Screaming in pain he replied: 'You can kill me if you want, but you will not find him here. He is gone away with his relatives somewhere, I don't know.'

'You don't know, don't you? If we find him here, this will be the last day on earth for both of you, mind that . . .' The men went inside the bedroom. In a corner huddled together were two women, clad in burquas. Without interrogating them the villains left the room and scoured the veranda, terrace, kitchen garden and left, threatening Jamal with dire consequences if he dared protect his friend.

After half-an-hour Jamal and Hassan went inside. Numb with fear were Sabina and Hamida, Jamal's mother and sister. As soon as the two men entered, Sachin lifted the veil of the burqua and appeared from the rear of an almirah, not visible to the attackers.

Next morning, before daylight, both the boys surreptitiously went to the mansion. They discovered Manindra, lying in a pool of blood, stone-dead, with a gash in his throat. They buried his body in the backyard of the mansion. After the incident Sachin went into hiding in an underground storeroom which had escaped the flames. There was clearly no other option but to immigrate. After a perfunctory completion of his father's funeral rites, he prepared to go to Calcutta. The house had been ransacked and valuables looted. There was no money, nothing to keep him back. Some Muslim sympathisers, who were still grateful to Manindra for his benevolence, collected some, for Sachin's migration to India. Before the day of departure the two boys met and promised to keep in touch. They exchanged whatever they had with them and burst into tears. Sachin left. But it was very difficult for him to communicate regularly. Postal vagaries made it impossible for letters to reach on time.

After Sachin's departure from his ancestral home, Hassan became unemployed. Jamal too was looking for work. For a brief period Sachin resided in one of his aunt's houses in Calcutta. He left suddenly, making it difficult for Jamal to locate him. In Calcutta, Sachin was moving from place to place to get a job. After months of infrequent communication, Sachin's letter arrived with the news of a satisfactory job in an import-export firm and of his permanent residence. Jamal wrote back with news that he had set up a tea-shop near his house and the death of his father. Then there was a long break between their epistolary exchanges. Jamal almost disappeared from Sachin's life. Sachin had no other alternative but to give up writing.

Scuttling through the tortuous tracks of life, Sachin's nostalgia for his homeland receded. Not that the memories of the last day at the estate were unmixed. His father's untimely and violent end, the destruction of the house of his forebears were blood-raw. But still there was no denying the recollections of his days with Jamal. His face often surfaced in his dreams. The deep set eyes rising above the tumultuous waters of the sea, then overwhelmed by a huge tidal wave of fury, left Sachin paralysed in his sleep.

In 1971, East-Pakistan became Bangladesh—an independent country. Sachin started harbouring hopes of Jamal's visit to India. There was nothing he could do to reach out to him. He received the staggering news that Chowdhury estate was razed to the ground. But Jamal, his Jamu, knew his address. Why didn't he write to him?

2005, an afternoon in Calcutta. A dark, stout, middle-aged man knocked the door of a small house in Kasba. It was a Sunday and Prabhat was home. He opened the door and saw a stranger waiting outside.

'Is this Mr. Sachindra Chowdhury's house?'

'Yes it is.'

'Can I speak to him? I have come a long way—from Bangladesh.'

'Why do you want to meet him?' Prabhat asked, curious.

'Are you Mr. Chowdhury's son?'

'I am.'

'Actually, I have something to give your father. My name is Iqbal Kader; my father's name is Jamaluddin Kader.' Recognition dawned on Prabhat's face. He had heard this name mentioned so many times!

'Please come in', he said.

Iqbal seemed restless and said that he had to rush home without delay.

'Why the hurry?'

'My father is dying. He has only a few days to live.'

'I am sorry to hear that. What has happened to him?'

'He has a liver disease. Last stage. The doctors have given up hope.' He continued in a grim manner, and related what he had heard from Jamal. Jamal, his three sons and wife had to flee to his uncle's house in

Nilhati in mid 1971, fearing assault by the Pakistani armed forces. Jamal had enlisted in the guerrilla army of the freedom-fighters and was subsequently maimed in the right arm in an encounter. After the freedom of Bangladesh, situations improved. Jamal set up a garment business in Nilhati and Iqbal with his two brothers was managing the business. He continued:

'My father has lately become extremely reticent. All he does is to stare at some letters. A week or two back he called me to him. Showing me your parents' photograph and address, he asked me to deliver them to him.'

Jamal's son rummaged his side-bag and brought out a parcel, wrapped in faded yellow newspaper and opened it. There were several letters written by Sachin, a photograph with his wife Nandita and a wristwatch. Iqbal continued, 'He took this watch with him even when he went to fight. Never for a single moment did he get it off his wrist.'

'Why has he returned it?'

'He has become crazy; hates all of us. Says we've made his life a hell. He doesn't want these things to be desecrated by our foul hands. They are so valuable that he wants to return them to the rightful owner before he dies.' Iqbal stopped for a while and sipped the drink offered.

'Now can I speak to Mr.Chowdhury please, and hand him these? He'll drive me nuts asking whether I've put the watch on his wrist or not.'

'Both my parents died five years ago.'

'Ya Allah! What am I to tell him then? The news sure will be a shock enough to kill him instantly!'

'You'll do nothing of the kind. You'll not tell uncle Jamal about my parents' deaths. Say that you've met them.' At that moment a fresh faced girl with two long plaits aged about twelve came inside the room and sat close to Prabhat.

'Your daughter I guess?'

'Yes.'

'Very pretty', said Iqbal, his eyes warm and soft.

'Do a namaskar (touch the feet of elders to show respect) to uncle Iqbal, Dolon'. The girl complied.

'I have two sons of my own.'

'They must be about my Dolon's age, isn't it?'

'One is eleven and the other, eight. Sabir and Salim.'

Time passed unnoticed in discussing the lives of their fathers. Iqbal seemed to forget that he was in a hurry. There was an arcane kinship that both felt for each other. Suddenly Prabhat remembered something and went out of the room. After a few minutes he entered with a faded parcel. Looking at it he remembered how curious he was when he saw Sachin shoving it under the clothes. Sachin had never revealed its contents. Never even to his wife.

'Time will come when you will have to open it', Sachin had said, when Prabhat asked him what it contained. He was shaken to discover how the words of his father had come true. It was an instinctive recognition on his part, of the moment that his father had indicated, at least thirty years before. 'How inexplicable things could be!' he mused. Prabhat unwrapped the decayed brown paper and exhibited the contents. Letters and only letters from Jamaluddin Kader! He had foolishly expected something else. A trifle dejected, he started folding them carefully. Then there was a faint tinkle. Dolon jumped from her seat and picked up something. An outdated one-paisa coin. She stared at it quizzically.

'This is it!' cried Prabhat with elation, when he saw it. Iqbal too understood the significance of the little object.

'Can I have this as a proof to show my father that I've been here? He has become so suspicious these days.'

'Of course you can. And take this as a remembrance.'

He took out a photograph of Dolon from his purse and handed it to Iqbal who asked for a piece of paper and wrote something on it.

'Here's my address in Bangladesh,' said Iqbal, handing the paper to Prabhat. Looking at Dolon's picture he smiled. 'Father is very fond of girls. It doesn't go well with him that there is none in our family. At least he'll die happy knowing that uncle Sachin has a beautiful grand-daughter.'

FROM THEIR OWN LIPS

The incident which I am about to relate was heard by me from the lips of those people who had experienced it. There is adequate evidence of the occurrence. It is an unexaggerated account of the real life encounter of those people who were alive only ten years ago. Doubts of verbal veracity do not arise since they were my close relations who were incapable of fabrication. For obvious reasons I have tried to keep their identity intact by not revealing their real names.

The incident which I am about to relate occurred in the early nineteen-forties in what was once East-Bengal; (the present day Bangladesh). Newly married couple Ranjan and Rakhi were living in a colossal mansion in Lalbag, Dacca. Ranjan was in business, and his very pretty wife Rakhi was a versatile singer. In those days marriage took place early. The groom was twenty-two and the bride, sixteen. In the early forties, Dacca wasn't like as it is now, a modern city. Lalbag was on the fringes of Dacca; totally undeveloped.

Ranjan and his younger brother Kumar inherited the estate after the demise of their parents. The house was remote, situated miles away from the town. Kumar lived in Dacca proper, where he was pursuing a degree in a college. He used to come to Lalbag often, especially during the holidays, to cheer up his sister-in-law, who felt extremely isolated when her husband went to work. Rakhi's gloomy days were lightened by his chatter and innumerable jokes. Both were very good friends.

During the day servants came to cook and do the household chores, and all of them left before nightfall. The reason was not inexplicable. Without electricity, the house looked formidable. Inside its dark womb were shadowy corners, niches, where sunlight refused to enter; narrow, labyrinthine corridors where one crossed with a sense of trepidation. The illiterate and superstitious servants were overawed. They would not reason. In large houses those uneasy places often existed. There was nothing unusual in that. But Rakhi made it a point to avoid those snaky interiors even during the day. It was not her fault. She was a mere child. An old woman named Sarala, who was very affectionate to her, succumbed to the couple's entreaties of keeping her company till Ranjan arrived.

Rakhi often heard whispers amongst the servants, which were stalled, the moment they espied her from a distance. Perturbed, she broached the subject to her husband.

'Is there something wrong somewhere in this house?'

'Why, what's happened?'

'The servants refuse to stay after six in the evenings, no matter how much I request them. They leave their jobs unfinished and disappear as quickly as they can'.

'These people, Rakhi, work the whole day. They naturally feel tired after the day's work.'

'But we are only two of us in this house!'

'Yes, but imagine the labour of keeping this huge mansion spruced up, washed etc., not to mention the gardening, cooking . . . .'

'But they rush away as if something was chasing them out of this house!' she said, childlike, but observant of everything around her.

'It's all your imagination. Comes from reading too many thrillers,' he smiled.

Rakhi was angry. Failing to convince her 'no-nonsense' husband, she cried, 'I am not joking. Besides, I don't read thrillers. Not in this house at least! I feel scared. There are six rooms downstairs, and I think I hear peculiar noises inside'.

'The rooms are always kept locked except on Sundays. Who would make noises?' Rakhi caught hold of another thread, nonchalantly.

'But I always sense someone behind me, especially when I enter the hall.'

'I told you it's all your imagination. Keep yourself occupied and you'll feel nothing', was the advice.

She felt hurt and retorted, 'Of course I keep myself occupied. Supervising the kitchen, picking flowers for puja, sewing, reading, practising my songs for the music teacher . . .'

'I know, I know, you don't have to elaborate.'

'I am not elaborating. I asked you a question and you have evaded it'. She pouted in dismay.

'Well don't be angry. There is nothing in this house to be scared of. We have been living here for generations; and I myself grew up here ever since I was a child. Besides, I can feel nothing. Nothing at all! There have been no complaints against this house from anyone till now.'

'May be it is a recent affair. That's why the servants leave early.'

Ranjan was irritated by his wife's logical persistence. 'Rakhi you are being unreasonable.'

'Am I? Are you sure?'

'Yes, definitely.'

Undeterred, his wife continued interrogating. 'But why do the servants stop talking amongst themselves whenever they see me?'

'Perhaps they criticise us, that's why.'

Unconvinced by his answers she persisted, 'Every day? But why? They have no reason to be. I don't even know how to scold them if they don't work.' Ranjan frowned; exasperated. Rakhi was being too importunate!

'Look Rakhi', he said, 'I am really tired. I don't want to repeat myself.'

Das mansion was a sprawling structure, surrounded by gigantic fruit trees of all kinds. From the huge tract of land which led to the garden, one could see the portico that led to the hall. In the evening, without the convenience of electricity, the gargantuan house would look forbidding, with dark shadows roaming all over its body. Beyond the precincts of the house were dense bushes and strange trees which cast weird shapes along the boundary wall. The evenings were astir by the jackals' nocturnal hunts and howls, reaching a choric crescendo, menacing enough to chill one's blood. But in villages at that time, it wasn't unusual at all! The ambience was uncomfortably disquieting but not uncanny.

All the rooms on the ground floor were generally locked. In the evening a lantern was placed on the portico for Ranjan's entry. Except for one or two rooms, everything was wrapped in darkness. Ranjan took the lantern upstairs to his bedroom. The estate was gigantic and there were no houses nearby. From a long distance one could view little flickering lights—possibly from the huts of the servants who worked in the house. In the morning the mansion would regain its former glory; glow in the sunshine and the chirp of the birds mixed with household noises would make it vibrant.

It was a Sunday. Kumar arrived before lunch and Rakhi had a fine time chatting with him. After lunch Ranjan preferred a short siesta. He enjoyed the way Rakhi massaged his bare back lightly till he fell asleep. She did it on her own accord when she was in the mood. It was summer and the heat was unbearable. Ranjan undid his shirt and lay down with his face to the wall of the bedroom. He heard Rakhi's voice saying, 'You go to sleep and I'll rub your back.' Rakhi went on with the massage and Ranjan soon fell asleep. After a while he said, 'Rakhi you woke me up.'

'I am so sorry', she said, and continued massaging.

Ranjan instantly fell asleep. After sometime Rakhi shook him and informed that a man was waiting for him downstairs. Disoriented by the vigorous shaking he received, he looked at her, bewildered. Smiling at him, he saw her leaving the room. Ranjan finished the meeting with his visitor and went upstairs, seething with rage. Seeing Rakhi and Kumar laughing and talking blithely, he spewed fire.

'How could you do this to me, Rakhi?' he queried. Both Rakhi and Kumar looked at each other, bewildered.

'What did I do?' she responded innocently. Kumar was astounded at the outburst.

'What's the matter Dada (brother)?'

'Just see what your Boudi (sister-in-law) did to me!'

'What?'

'Scratched my back, black and blue. I can't see but I think it's lacerated. It's burning like hell!'

Both Kumar and Rakhi looked at each other, stupefied!

'Why, when?' asked Kumar.

'Why, when? Didn't Rakhi go to my room to massage my back?'

'Boudi?'

'Yes, your Boudi. Didn't she go there, and a few minutes ago tell me that there was a man calling me downstairs?'

'Dada, listen. Boudi didn't budge from this room from the time you went to sleep. We were conversing together!'

'Conversing together! You too Kumar are lying to me?'

'O god! Why should I?'

'I don't believe it. Ask Rakhi! I saw her with my own eyes!'

Poor Rakhi was crying. She couldn't make her husband believe in her and now both the brothers were debating over something that didn't happen!

Kumar finally said, 'Ok, if you don't believe us then there is nothing we can do!'

'Don't try to shield her Kumar, I saw her with my own eyes! I felt her hands on my back, I heard her voice. Do you think I am a nut-case; a daydreamer? If so, why is my back searing as if it had been burnt?'

He took off his shirt and turned around for them to see. The revelation was a shock. On Ranjan's back were horrible lacerations, red, swollen and bloody. No words could describe the terrible sight! It looked as if long fingernails were dug into the flesh, trying to draw blood. There were dark red lines which started from the neck to the waist, and all along Ranjan was in a trance!—In the depths of sleep! Consciousness of the intense pain occurred after he went to talk to the visitor downstairs.

The only question that irked Ranjan was how he could go on sleeping when he was being mauled! But he did not utter a word.

Seeing the scars, Rakhi and Kumar shrieked together. Ranjan had to be shown the wounds and a doctor consulted immediately. A long mirror, set on an almirah in front and a small one at the rear, illustrated the terrifying outrage staged on his bare back. Ranjan had to admit that no human hand could cause such slashes on the skin, least of all a woman's. And why would his wife hurt him so? At last convinced, he thought for a moment, his flesh creeping; and cried out in horror, 'What was it?'

Rakhi at last had proved her point.

LOVE

Alok and Kabita lived in a small flat with their son Rishi and his grandmother, who was widowed at a very early age. She was a primary school teacher with a meagre salary which she spent in raising her son and running the house. Her husband having died young had left her nothing. Maya worked relentlessly and brought up Alok with no one to look forward to for succour. Alok worked as an insurance agent and married Kabita who was a receptionist in a private firm. Both their income sufficed to cover the household expenses but left them with very little to fall back on.

When Rishi was born, Maya took the responsibility of her grandson who warmed the core of her heart. She hardly had time for herself. Looking after a new-born baby was a tough job especially at the age of sixty. Added to that pleasurable pain were household chores which drained her by early evening. Alok worked extra hard, to meet the expenses of the child who grew up healthy and strong, while his granny's constitution withered. Both the child and Maya were inseparable. In the evenings when the parents came home he preferred to do his homework with Maya who devoted as much time as possible to her grandchild. During holidays too the boy would have nothing to do with his mother. Kabita tried mollycoddling Rishi into accepting her but her son was immune to all her strategic advances of gaining his confidence. He grew up to be a boy of five and would hang on to his granny whom he called 'mum'.

Kabita felt slighted by her son. There was an intense relationship with Maya which was difficult for her to sever. She tried zealously to obviate the factors which distanced her from Rishi. Alok tried to reason with her.

'It's natural that he would take to mother since she is the one who is bringing him up. All children are specially attached to their grandparents. They become their friends.'

'No, the point is not attachment to her, but detachment from me. Alok, I am his mother. He should take to me naturally, which he doesn't. This is odd.'

'Well, I'm his father am I not? I don't make a fuss about it! Rishi is too young to differentiate between a parent and a grandparent. It's natural that he is fond of the one with whom he spends most of his time. Besides, do you even acknowledge the trouble mother takes for him, at her age; bringing up a child, not to mention running the house? You should thank your stars for such a mother-in-law! You only criticise instead of being grateful! She's getting weak day by day! Have you ever noticed that! Look at her life! She's brought me up single-handedly, against all odds, and is still working to keep us free from worries. Do you ever appreciate that?'

Kabita was more than adequately reprimanded. Silenced, she knew whatever Alok was saying was true. But inwardly, she vowed never to be estranged from her son. She thought of devious ways to get rid of Maya. Knowing full well about Alok's non-cooperation in this matter, Kabita did not immediately take steps but heaped heavier work-burden on her, grumbling and fussing about trivial mistakes. Maya did not retort but went on doing passively what she could do, to avoid disputes.

Dreadfully tired after work she had to entertain the child with stories till he fell asleep on her lap. The parents had insisted that he sleep with them, but the child flatly refused.

'I will sleep with mum, she tells me stories'.

'I will tell you stories too Rishi,' his mother responded.

'But they are never as good as mum's.'

In spite of his parents' efforts Maya and Rishi remained inextricably connected. But things were taking a turn for the worse. Burdened with responsibilities and work she frequently fell ill. Kabita's plan was working; and working fast. She broached the subject of Maya's illness to Alok, her words masked with concern.

'Mother is getting weaker and weaker, poor thing. I think we'll have to keep a twelve-hour maid who will cook and look after Rishi.'

Alok was working and Kabita had broached the subject at an opportune moment. Absently, he agreed to the proposal, unable to gauge her intention. She had been gathering information from care-centres and within a week a maid was recruited.

Yet Maya's health deteriorated, but she had to humour the demanding child.

One day Maya fell so ill that it was not possible any longer for her to get up from the bed. She was reluctant to go to a hospital and a nurse was required. Alok was certain that it was well nigh impossible for him to keep both a nurse and maid. He was in a quandary. Guessing the problem Maya called her son.

'I understand the trouble you are facing Alok. I know it is impossible for you to keep a nurse for me.'

'No mother . . . don't worry, we'll manage.'

'Maya calmly responded, 'I know you will son, but it will be a great economic strain on you. Rishi is growing up, you need money for him.'

'So what? Shall I let you die without nursing you?'

'No, that's not what I meant. I have an idea'.

'What?'

'Send me to my nephew's 'Raksha', the old people's home. He won't charge much, and my pension will cover the expenses. There are doctors on call the whole day. I'll be constantly monitored and you will not have to be anxious about me, as you are now, since both you and Kabita stay away from home most of the time. I will be much less of a worry for you.'

'But Rishi? Have you thought about him?'

'Rishi needs to be separated from me. I am old and can die any moment. That will be a greater shock to him. It's time he's weaned from me to get closer to his parents.'

Alok didn't answer. He acknowledged to himself that his mother was right. It was time Rishi came closer to them. Kabita heard about the conversation with quiet elation. She kept her feelings to herself and did not venture an answer that may spoil her plans.

Maya revived a little and preparations were surreptitiously made for her departure so as not to arouse Rishi's suspicion. As he left for school, Maya, weeping profusely started for her new home. All that was old was trivial now, except her husband's photograph and the little child, to whom she had given her soul.

In 'Raksha', Maya viewed her surroundings. She felt it was worse than death. Old, old, old faces . . . She had felt a child's nimble hands on her heart and spirit and was awash with the springtime hues of a garden when the evening's crimson sun settles on it. Here there were dried up trees awaiting the final countdown. She longed for a caress of the two little hands to drench her thirsted soul. She couldn't survive in that hell, she knew.

Rishi came home from school. Strangely, his parents were present that day. Evading both, he ran to his granny's room. He shouted for her. There was no answer. He had not taken a liking to the new maid who tried to impress him. He pushed her away refusing to be fed or clothed by her, preferring his grandmother instead. When Maya was ill he would sit by her and kiss her from time to time watching intently whether the kisses lessened her illness or not. Without screaming he ate and dressed in front of his 'mum'. Where was she? Why didn't she answer? Why were his parents looking at him so queerly?

'Where is mum?' he shouted at Kabita.

'Mum is gone to a relative's house. She'll be back after a few days', she answered with trepidation.

'Who will feed me, clothe me?'

'Why Rakhi will, dear!'

'Rakhi! I hate her!'

'Today I'm home. I'll feed you darling!'

'No. Where's my mum?'

'I told you she'll come back.'

'Is she dead? Dead people don't come back.'

'Oh! No Rishi, don't say this! She's okay.'

'You've sent her away somewhere, I know! I hate you.'

Kabita was angry. She slapped Rishi hard on the face and told him to change and have lunch; otherwise he would be facing grievous consequences.

'My mum never slapped me', he wailed. 'You're wicked, you've sent her away. I won't eat or change,' Rishi instinctively reacted.

The whole day passed without Rishi taking a bite. Relentless crying had made him weak. He refused to go to school having nothing to do with either of his parents who had to stay back from work and fought with one another. Alok's vituperations left Kabita stunned.

'This is your doing. Your subtle manoeuvres! Racing to defeat mother! And now your son hates you even more. You couldn't take things naturally, you couldn't.'

Kabita reacted contemptuously, 'What about you? You talk as if I had done the whole thing. Why did you let her go? You, the good son!'

Meanwhile Maya lying in a small cramped room awaited death. She was suffocating in the dingy room with another old woman who was mentally challenged. She remembered only the moments with the little one, trying to probe how he would react in her absence. Her last days she surmised, would end only with the sweetest remembrances of her grandchild.

Rishi, after being assaulted by his mother declined to eat and had to be physically coerced to do so. He lay in a delirium asking for Maya.

'Mum I want to hear the story of the princess and the frog', he mumbled. His agony moved his parents to tears.

Gradually the child had to succumb to the pangs of hunger. He started eating, going to school and maintaining his routined existence. Weeks elapsed, as Rishi calmed down, to the relief of his parents. His docility reassured them. Weeks passed. A letter from the class-teacher of his school was delivered one day through Rishi, requesting a meeting with his parents. To their surprise the teacher did not focus on his studies but seemed worried about his conduct which she thought had undergone a radical transformation. It was not a complaint but an observation on her part that the boy who was usually very agile and playful had become very quiet. Even during play-time he refused to go out with his friends as was his habit. She sensed that something that irked him, was preying upon his usual activities. It was her analysis that Rishi was psychologically upset about something he did not reveal. The parents looked at each other knowingly, dismissing the version of the teacher as 'baseless'. Things began to fall in place, to Alok and Kabita's satisfaction. They even began to suspect that Maya's over-indulgence had turned their son into a recalcitrant and disobedient individual. The child complied with everything asked of him. He slept with his parents, was not resentful or snappish, and was extraordinarily quiet. Alok, who was cool-headed and logical, began to believe that Maya's departure was more beneficial to Rishi than he had anticipated. He did his duty by enquiring about his mother's health over the phone. His wife was right. He had misunderstood her. Things were as they should have been. Kabita, a twister had mutated to a handy stone which had knocked out three birds. Rishi was now her son and only her son; she had gained Alok's confidence and had succeeded in getting his devouring mother out of the way! But one thing seemed to appear unnatural to her. Rishi really did not respond to any show of love by his parents. Toys remained untouched, caresses unreciprocated. Rishi behaved like an automaton. Kabita thought of the class-teacher's words. Yet she was reluctant to acknowledge her own fear or tell her husband about it. The couple dared not venture to take Rishi to 'Raksha'. They were scared of raking up the ashes of the past.

Days dragged on to months and Maya gave up hopes of any chance of a better life. She forced to accommodate herself physically and mentally to the ambience around her. Her thoughts did not centre on Alok and Kabita, though in the deepest recesses of her mind there was a lurking hope that Alok might visit her. She could not fathom the drastic change in her son who she thought was intensely attached to her. Maya abandoned these despairing thoughts and tried to veer them into reminiscences of her days with Rishi. She longed to hug her grandchild to her breast and weeping, said to herself,

'I will never see him again.'

Maya had given up hopes of a meeting; she reconciled herself to believing that the world is a weird place where everything that you have never dreamt of could happen. The most certain thing is death and she was waiting for it.

On a Sunday morning, Maya was asked to go to the lounge, for she had visitors. Helped by an attendant she went there, trembling with expectation. As soon as she entered, there was a storm. A rush of footsteps and two embracing hands were around her waist. The impact of this gesture destabilised Maya. She looked down at the teary-joyful face looking up to her in anticipation as she hugged him and made him sit on her lap like before. The child rested his head on her shoulders and cried as if his heart would break. After pacifying him, she tried to talk to Alok but was stopped by her grandson. In a loud voice he shouted, 'Mum, mum, mum come home. I will look after you now.' Encircling the child, Maya rested her head on his shoulder to hide the uncontrollable rain drenching her thirsted soul.

HOPE

Every day at 6 o'clock Malati and her friends caught the Canning local, bound for Calcutta and dispersed at various locations. All of them worked as charwomen till afternoon, except Malati, who slaved without a break, subsisting on the food given by her employers. She usually returned home at nine at night. In an hour she prepared dinner and waited for Pradip, her son, a student in a night college in Calcutta. Malati had no days-off except in exigencies. She lived in one of the many shanties in Canning consisting of a room and a common toilet. Her husband had left her and Pradip ten years before, stealing whatever money she had saved over the years. He absconded with another married woman, wallowing in the complacency of the success of the feat he accomplished without a furore. Malati had to work like a demon after that. Pradip worked half-a-day in a tea-shop to pay for his education, but that wasn't enough. Malati took everything in her stride because most of her friends experienced more or less the same predicament. The most important thing was that Pradip was studying in a college and was extremely attached to his mother. Her only dream was to educate him, in order to leap over the dismal pecuniary condition they were forced to face.

Inwardly, Malati was proud of Pradip's achievements in school and college. He was a solitary aspirant for a Bachelor's degree, among her friends' children. Travelling together, her co-workers often remarked that she was extremely lucky. Their children hardly cared about studies. Most of them were drop-outs from school and spent their time hobnobbing with local hooligans.

"Malati has a gem of a son. Apart from working he still is continuing his studies," they expressed their admiration.

"I have forgotten everything his father did, because of him," was Malati's rejoinder.

"Our husbands are either drunks or womanizers. Yet the children don't have any sympathy for us. We are slaving day in and day out without respite, only for them. They are turning out to be like their fathers", sighed another.

"I hope Pradip doesn't change". Malati's expression was tinged with conviction to the contrary.

"No, he is not that sort. He helps you. He is educated—not like our sons. From his very childhood he was different. Such a quiet, unassuming boy! We've been observing him for so many years!"

Malati's heart expanded with the accolades Pradip received. The heat, the crowd inside the train, seemed so tolerable! She would work even harder if need be, to push him up higher in the social rung. She had saved a little money to celebrate Pradip's twentieth birthday. It was a Friday and she decided to invite two of her closest friends. On the previous night she took pains to prepare the vegetables and fish she wished to cook. She took the day-off from the various houses except that of one; an elderly couple who were totally dependent on her. Pradip was given a new shirt that day by his mother. His breakfast was of payasam, a sweet delicacy specially prepared for auspicious occasions.

Malati decided to go to a temple to pray and gift flowers to the deity for her son's welfare. Mother and son both decided to return early that day. After finishing cooking, she said,

"Pradip, don't stay back late today. I've invited aunt Deepa and Bela".

"Why mother, why do you want to spend your hard-earned money like this? Can we afford the luxury?"

"No, I had saved some money for your birthday. I have never done anything for you; no new clothes, no good shoes-nothing. It's my wish that I celebrate your birthday this year. But you must be back home by five o'clock". Then with a pause, she said,

"I really wish you were at home today".

"Ma, I can't. I won't go to college, but to a hostel in Calcutta. I am going to get some notes, for my exams."

"But you could go tomorrow."

"No Ratul will not come to college from today. He will be studying for the exam and will leave the hostel tomorrow and go home."

"I understand. But . . . . ."

"Don't worry; I will be home by five o'clock."

Malati returned home at three in the afternoon. She changed the torn bedcover and spruced up the room for her two guests. But she felt uneasy. Inside the train to Canning she had heard several people grumbling for being late. There was an accident in the afternoon local for Calcutta which caused the delay in the arrival of the down train. One passenger remarked,

"It had to be today. I had an urgent work at home."

"Poor chap, tried to cross the line. Didn't notice the signal".

"This is how they put their lives at stake. What's the hurry!"

"Crossing the over-bridge was too much!" quipped another.

"Do you know what happened to this guy?"

"No, he was sent to the hospital-I reckon".

"No chance of survival?".

"Can't say."

Malati ruminated. Pradip should have been here by now. She readied the flowers, the grass (for the ritual), the sweets and the lamp. Then she placed a worn-out rug for her son to sit on.

"God, let this boy survive," she prayed. Then she brushed aside the wretched thoughts. Wasn't she celebrating Pradip's birthday today!

The news came at five in the evening. She was to go to a hospital in Calcutta. It was none else but Pradip who in a hurry to go early to his friend's house met with the accident. It was serious. For a moment Malati was dumbstruck. Tears didn't come. There was a trembling in her bones. She accompanied two of her friends she had invited. Pradip's friends too went; ready to give their blood if necessary. Throughout the journey Malati watched the posters of the latest films, posters of political parties, boys, girls, students in uniforms. In the suffocating heat and the insouciant crowd she stood still, her eyes vacant. She felt left alone in a field, being dragged by someone unknown, someone whose face was hidden. She longed to see that face eluding her, but couldn't. Peering outside, Malati saw ponds, ducks, children playing in the mud; so intently that it seemed she was seeing them for the first time in her life.

She reached the hospital. The operation was in progress. Malati gathered that there would have been a head-on collision if Pradip in a flash, didn't throw himself down on the tracks, keeping his head out of the rails. There wasn't any time to move away his hands before a thousand voices were drowned in the deafening rumble that crossed over him. He felt the cutting edge of the wheels on his hands. But he didn't budge, knowing that it would be sheer death. He was still conscious when the local people rescued him and took him to the hospital.

"Please inform my mother. I mayn't survive. She lives in Canning-her name is Malati Mondol," was what he could utter before being dragged into oblivion. All around Malati, were discussions about his son.

"I can hardly imagine a cool-tempered boy like him doing such a thing—crossing the tracks without noticing the signal . . ."

"He said, he was to go home quickly today. His mother would be waiting."

"What a boy! My God, I would have had a heart-attack then and there before the train sliced me off!"

"Yes, extremely courageous; God grant he survives".

"He may, if the operation is successful, but there is no guarantee".

She stood stock-still, listening. Pradip's friends requested her to sit, but she seemed to hear nothing. Malati looked at the faces, the people going to and fro, nurses, doctors, medicine-counter queue; patients on wheel-chairs being led out, patients in stretchers being led in, helpers, maids, elevators . . . . , a body made ready for the funeral, relatives mourning their loss; the mad rush of visitors, interminable series of images. Like a voodoo doll she perambulated under the control of some inexplicable force coercing her into imbibing everything. The smell of rectified spirit, medicines, people waiting, announcements on the microphone, many anxious looks, happy recoveries—cries of pain . . . . the terrifying threshold of life and death. Malati was deaf to the consolations of her friends. She did not court them; waiting instead for something else. Hours passed without her sitting down or asking for help.

It took three hours for the operation to be over. Blood was necessary. His friends had volunteered. The doctor came out to meet his relatives.

"Where is the boy's mother?" he queried. Malati instantaneously jerked herself out of her strange reticence. Looking at him in the eye the first thing she uttered was,

"Doctor is my son alive?"

"He is, but I am sorry to say that he would never be able to use his hands. The right arm is gone and the left palm badly tattered had to be amputated" Malati looked away, then she reiterated,

"Just tell me that he will survive, that his life is not in danger."

"That I can assure you, if things suddenly do not take a drastic change for the worse which is unlikely, since he is responding well after the operation. It will take about a month for him to recover fully. From what I heard all credit goes to him. You have a brave boy. He has cheated death and he will overcome this handicap".

"So, he will survive; that's what I want to know," persisted Malati, who now bypassed the accolades of her son, she so loved to hear.

"He will, definitely. And you should be proud of him for defying a certain death." She was mute.

After sometime, she was allowed to see her son from a distance. She saw only bandages, oxygen and other medical equipments around him.

"You will live my son, you will. I'll be the two hands you have lost." Malati wept at last.

NISHA'S SECRET

She rummaged the kitchen drawer for the knife. Gripping the hard plastic handle, she felt exhilarated. It was exactly what she wanted. After years of slaving she had come to a decision. As soon as he would ring the bell, enter the room, she would just have to thrust it inside his bulging belly. Then a gushing red would spill out on the floor of her bedroom. The vision thrilled her. She pictured herself outside the house, then getting in and screaming for help. Nisha sighed with a sense of satisfaction. The doorbell rang. With a sense of anticipation she moved to the door, trembling inside. Opening it, she saw to her dismay, the grocer with the list of purchases made. The grocer ensconced himself complacently on the floor and slowly one by one read out the items she had bought. Nisha fuming with anger, clenched her teeth and told him to hurry, but the latter ignored her and continued reading the list of three months' unpaid bills. She gritted her teeth.

'Lousy old man! Had to come now, at this particular moment.'

The doorbell rang a second time. This time it was Mahesh, her husband. The grocer opened the door. Quickly she shoved the knife under the table cloth. Mahesh stared. She was caught. He accosted her.

'Look at the amount of money you have been spending,' he roared, looking at the bills. The grocer scuttled away without the money. He was terribly scared of Mahesh, who told him to come the following week.

Nisha trembled with fear. That fear which was eating up her life. Mahesh continued belligerently,

'What were you hiding under the table-cloth? Don't think I didn't see it.'

'Er, it is just a new kitchen knife I had bought. The old one has become rusty.'

'Has it?' he laughed aloud. 'What is it doing here?' Taking the knife out from its hiding place he looked at it.

'Better keep it in a safe place.' He opened his own drawer, put the knife inside and locked it. Nisha wanted to scream. The ordeal would begin again she knew.

Like every other day he said, 'Bring me my clothes and be sure to polish my shoes before you go to bed.' As she worked, anger replaced tears.

'I shall turn him into a picture! I really shall,' she promised herself. Nisha thought of devious ways of finishing off her husband. She could do a Lorena Bobbitt! But no, the knife was gone! She hated the movement of his hulk over her; as if she was making love to a cement mixer, churning, rotating endlessly, probing her in a way which made her feel that all her secrets lay huddled between her legs! Added to that was the arrogance of thinking that he was the sole authority in manipulating her and none else! The elation of possessing a body! Disgusting! She detested every inch of that man! Dominating, commanding, possessive, selfish to the core! Yet it wasn't possible for her to leave him, for she neither had friends nor relatives who would shelter her. Nisha thought of various implements and methods of freeing herself from that despicable creature! Nothing seemed very practical. One of her most original ideas was to overpower Mahesh with an overdose of sleeping pills, then tie his legs and hang him upside down from the hook of the ceiling-fan like an oversized mutton. But the monstrous weight of the man, would be too much for her to handle. So she gave up the idea. Rat-poison perhaps? It may be a decent try. But then the police would soon hound her out since she was the one who cooked for him! She had read plenty of murder-mystery stories. But they were of no use, now that she needed help.

It was a routine for Mahesh to check things which were unlocked, every day before he left for the office and before he went to bed. Except for her clothes' wardrobe and kitchen cabinets, everything else was under lock and key. Every night Mahesh would also inspect the bed before dozing off and not close his eyes till she was in deep slumber. If Nisha woke up in the middle of the night to go to the washroom, she would discover him sitting bolt upright on the bed waiting for her!

The suffocating presence of her husband became intolerable to Nisha. On Sundays, she imagined herself a chicken inside a coop, beating its wings. Strangely enough, Mahesh, unlike other days, seemed relaxed and passive. He refrained himself from any sort of interrogation or inspection relating to his wife and gave her the full liberty to do as she wished. But his wife knew better. She interpreted his innocuous behaviour as a veneer, to catch her on the wrong foot! She wasn't a nut-case as he supposed! These ruminations only augmented her torment while Mahesh remained cool and collected enjoying himself. Sometimes he proposed to take her to the movies. She complied half-heartedly because he inevitably walked her back home through those streets she hated to go. Nisha thought that plaguing her, gave Mahesh a sadistic pleasure. He was a free-wheeling pervert! Yet she could not deny that her husband took care that she ate and dressed well and took days off from office and nursed her back to health when she was ill. But still she was on a psychic leash. That was searing agony! There was no escaping it! None would give her a job, for she was past forty and did not have the required qualifications for it. Nor would anybody shelter her since she was penniless! To escape was to kill, and to kill means freedom! As days passed, Nisha's determination soared.

It was a Sunday afternoon. Mahesh was asleep and Nisha was watching television. A neighbour with whom she was friendly, dropped by. During the conversation, Nisha unravelled her misery to Mala. It was a shocking eye-opener to the latter because Mahesh was well respected as a gentleman; in good terms with everyone in the neighbourhood. But why would Nisha lie about her husband! The hatred was so intense that she was hell-bent on killing him! Nisha's voice rose in enthusiastic fury when she was narrating her plight to Mala. She had closed the door of Mahesh's room from where his snoring assured her that he was fast asleep. Meanwhile she was off the hook and raised her voice in unrestrained passion.

'I shall be the end of that fiend! I shall!'

'But that would be foolish. You would have to go to jail! Don't you understand that?' Mala cautioned her.

'I'll run away before they find me out!'

'Don't be so dumb. There are other ways to become free than killing. To escape one domestic prison you'll land on another which will make you think that the former was a paradise!'

'What will I do then?'

'Seek a divorce, that's all!'

'Don't think that I haven't thought about it. He won't give me the consent. He is so damned possessive! Besides, where would he get an unpaid servant?'

'Then seek a lawyer's advice.'

'Who would give me the money? He takes care to see that I don't have any extra money. Even if I happen to have some, he worms it out of me.'

'Why, it's impossible to believe he is such a rogue!'

Mala thought of the various possible ways of her friend's emancipation. Suddenly a thought struck her. She eagerly caught hold of her friend's hands and almost shouted, 'Well, why hadn't I thought of that before?'

'What?'

'Why, the women's cell. We can inform them! In fact I have a friend who is a member of that organisation. It is called WWO (Women's Welfare Organisation). It listens to the problems of women and tries to address them. They could easily handle your case.'

Nisha was so delighted that she forgot to check in on her husband who had meanwhile opened the door when the two friends were conversing, and had imbibed every single word that was said. As soon as he heard that Mala was to bring her friend with her next Sunday at four o'clock in the afternoon, he quietly closed it and went to bed. He was not interested in knowing anything more.

Mala departed and Nisha sighed with pleasure to find the door still closed. The next day passed as usual. Tuesday arrived, but Mahesh showed no intention of going to the office. When accosted by his wife, he said that he had taken leave from work that week. Nisha did not question him any further in this matter and kept silent. Mahesh appeared to be extremely relaxed and did not keep an eye on her movements.

It was Sunday morning and Mahesh seemed to be very busy inside his bedroom. His wife went on with the usual chores. After lunch, Mahesh, unobserved left the house. Nisha was in the drawing room waiting for the auspicious moment of Mala and her friend's arrival. She was blithely assured that Mahesh was inside his room as usual taking a nap. A few minutes after four p.m. the duo arrived. After the preliminary introductions, Mala briefly narrated Nisha's woes and the life she was being forced to live in. The lady from WWO suggested that she talk with Mahesh. Nisha got up with feeling of trepidation, to her husband's room. The bed was bare; the closets and drawers in which he kept his valuables were open and empty. Nisha was in a state of shock. She went near the bed and found an envelope on top of which was written 'To whom it may concern.' She took the envelope, her heart beating fast with anticipation, and hurried to the ladies, stating Mahesh's disappearance. The lady from the women's cell started reading the letter.

'You have perhaps no idea why I am writing this letter to you. It is not cowardice which has forced me to leave this house, where I spent thirty years of my life. To be frank, I am accountable to no one but circumstances have taken such a turn that it makes me feel that I should narrate the truth. My wife and I were mentally estranged from each other, shortly after our marriage. To make matters clearer to you, I now take the liberty of unravelling the story of our conjugal life. I was thirty-five years old, a bachelor and without any parents when I first met Nisha. I worked as a cashier in a bank where I was respected for my sincerity and honesty. One day when I was returning home from Park Circus, I suddenly heard two voices—a man and a woman's. I had worked late that night and then went over to my friend's house where I was invited for dinner. It was almost eleven p.m. at night in December, and the streets were absolutely deserted. At other times I would have ignored the two quarrelling voices. But as fate would have it, I could not remain uninvolved that very night. The man's voice was commanding and stern while the woman's was that of terrible misery and despair. 'Please help me!' the woman cried as I passed by her and I stopped in my tracks. The woman (a street-walker I presumed by her dress and make-up) complained that the man with whom she was living had thrown her out on the streets, to fend for herself. I confronted him. He told me not to listen to her tales for she was a prodigious liar. Seeing her in such dire straits I took pity and requested him to give her shelter for that night at least. But he staunchly refused to listen to me. 'You don't know what she is. She's drained me dry. Scheming slut! She can very well spend the night without help! It has been three years and now I can no longer take it.' Saying this he walked away. Dear madam, to this day I remember each word the man had said twenty years ago. They are scorched in my memory. Now, for the rest of the narrative. I was left with a helpless girl in my hands in the middle of the night. I, as a human being could not leave her in the lurch. But looking back, I think I was the greatest fool in the world! I could have been kinder to myself, if I had not been kind to her!

I was respected in my neighbourhood for my impeccable character and taking her with me to my house would mean tarnishing my reputation. But at that moment I could do nothing but help a woman in distress. I gave her the night-shelter on condition that she left early in the morning the next day. She agreed. After that many mornings came and went but she refused to budge. I had no other option. If I asked her to go she would scream and rant and bring the house down. My respectability was at stake as neighbours became inquisitive and started talking about my degradation as a man of honour; yet god knows I had not touched the tip of her little finger. I was a trapped man. The only way left to me was to marry her, which was what she wanted. After our marriage, my life became a nightmare. She wormed away my money and her demands grew, till all I had saved over the years was almost gone. Her inordinate lust for jewellery and clothes knew no bounds. Reasoning with her was fruitless. She took the keys of my drawer in my absence and took out whatever she could. Barely two months had gone after our marriage before I realised that I was married to a vampire bat, bent on sucking out my life-blood. Yet I forgave her past, tried to console myself that her actions were the result of poverty and deprivation; and that she would gradually be able to love me. But all my assumptions were wrong. Not only financially, I felt drained out psychologically too. Her conduct haunted me like a nightmare and I began to make unpardonable errors at my workplace. At first I was warned by the authorities, who were accommodating, but by the end of my third year with her, I lost my job. I was totally broke. I tried to support ourselves by doing odd jobs. I told Nisha that I was unemployed, but she didn't heed my words and continued her life as before.

When reasoning and remonstrance failed, I decided that this must come to a stop. I exercised my hold on household expenses and the assets like jewellery, in order to curb her insatiable greed. Meanwhile, I got another job and was determined not to let it go by satisfying her whims and fancies. Dear madam, I hope you will realise the conditions which made me take resort to such means. I was fooled once and I would not let her fool me any longer. I dismissed the servant, thinking that hard work will keep her mentally occupied and tame her indomitable spirit. Physically, I was a man enough not to abuse her but I admit that my harsh and unrelenting behaviour was fruitful in a way. She had not seen the other side of me, and took me for granted. But now I began to exert my power, as I thought fit. But that step had a contrary effect. Unable to satisfy her terrible desire for money, she secretly planned to kill me! You can now imagine what I was going through! Every single day I was in fear for my life! I searched everything before I went to bed and could not rest till I saw her beside me! If you have any doubts about the veracity of my accusation, please ask madam Mala for corroboration. Nisha had already taken her into confidence. I had endured enough! With great apologies may I state that I am scared of women's institutions. I may be wrong, but I think that they have a preconceived notion that a woman is always a victim and not a predator. I know that her tearful words of my exploitation will surely move you to take steps against me. Therefore this letter. Before you judge me I thought I would relate the circumstances which led me on to being harsh and cruel with my wife. I don't know how much this letter will convince you, for she is a liar incarnate. When I heard that you were coming on Sunday, I had already made a decision. I have no money left to consult a lawyer or give her a divorce. So madam, the wisest thing I could do is leave, and leave for good. I have taken with me the moveable objects such as money, jewellery etc.—for I have to survive. I have found a job outside Calcutta, by god's grace, where my wife will never be able to get hold of me even by extending her long tentacles. I have left her the house, the deed of the house, giving her the full authority to do whatever she pleases with it.I have also left some cash which would last her more than a month or so. I consider myself a free man now. As for my wife, you may judge her as you please. Thanking you, Mahesh Chatterjee.'

The lady looked up at Nisha. 'Is it true?' she said.

Nisha's eyes flamed with contempt and fury. She screamed, 'He took away my jewels, the dust-bin!'

Mala and the lady looked at each other. 'Off her rocker. Needs to see a shrink', they concurred.

THE CIRCLE

After many years he woke up before dawn. A subtle discomfort was breaking his generally cream-rimmed sleep. Shuvo got up from the bed and stood on the balcony. It was half-past three and darkness loomed large over the neighbourhood. In the sky, winked a billion stars, sporting a silver spangled black coverlet, he almost forgot having seen in his student days.

The coverlet then turned to purple, embellished with the sequined glow of starlets. He was still standing, trying to recall the day's events which woke him up at an odd hour. Soon sparks of orange obliterated the gleaming clusters and spread its opulence across the sky. It brightened, as realisation dawned on him. Yes, he had met Mita a few days ago, and they were to meet that very day! She was once his classmate when they were studying in Presidency College. Shuvo, now a marketing manager in a multinational firm, was an eligible bachelor of thirty-eight. Mita, the same age as Shuvo, was a divorcee, a sales executive in a reputed company. Shuvo recalled the moment when he spotted her at the Park Street metro station a few days earlier, jostled forward by the rushing crowd. Instinctively he called out to her, and she looked back.

'Shuvo isn't it?'

'Yes, how are you Mita?'

'Ok.' She was still pretty, though a little more plump, which suited her very well.

'Well Shuvo, it's a long time since we met,' she replied, moving away from the crowd.

'More than a decade.'

'How could you spot me from afar?'

'I could, it needs no elaboration.'

'Still the same old Shuvo, you haven't changed.'

'Are you married?' the words were spontaneously out before he could control them.

'Was—now a divorcee.'

'Children?'—Again? Thought Shuvo, biting his lips.

'No, the marriage didn't last a year!'

'Oh! I'm sorry!'

'Nothing to be sorry about!' she continued in the same cheeky tone.

'And you?'

'An old bachelor.'

'Why? You're still handsome!'

'No particular reason. Didn't feel like marrying.'

Both discussed their workplaces, their goals, and their future. They decided to meet on a Sunday.

That Sunday that woke him up. The sky was a loud crimson. The morning walkers were up and about. Sounds of everyday life became more pronounced. But Shuvo stood still, drowning in the still grey waters of the past.

It was the last year in the university when Shuvo proposed to Mita. All over him trembled the blushing fluids of anticipation, of reciprocation. He had looked deep into her eyes; there were convincing signs of response. It made him feel confident. Shuvo was never verbose. He recited his proposal over and over again before venturing towards Mita. But it never happened. All around them were friends; gossiping, lecturing, showing off, to impress the girls.

However an opportunity arrived in the form of torrential rain. As Shuvo was entering the gate of the university, he spotted Mita standing under an awning of a book shop, waiting for the outpouring to stop. Luckily he had an umbrella with him that day. There were no friends around. As he approached, it seemed to Shuvo that she felt a sense of relief, being escorted by him. They hurried together under the umbrella to the university. Both decided to have coffee in the canteen before going to class. Mita looked stunning with shining beads of raindrops across her cheeks and forehead. Shuvo wished she wouldn't rub them off with her hanky, but she did. The deep sea of her eyes, looked calm, bereft of ripples. Coffee was served. With great trepidation, Shuvo blurted out the words which would haunt him throughout his life.

'Mita, let me tell you something if you permit me to.'

'What is it?'

'I love you madly, intensely!'

She kept quiet. The sea in the eyes spurted out ripples. The ripples became huge tides—tearing the shore.

'Have you come to help me out in the rain just to tell me this?'

'No, no, Mita, I met you by accident, not to take any advantage.'

'By accident, is it? How dare you lie to me!'

'My god, is it wrong to love someone and declare it?'

'Yes.' She was recalcitrant. Inconsiderate.

'Don't say this to me again,' she hissed audaciously and left the room. Shuvo sat there stunned. Minutes, hours, passed by. The cooled layered coffee remained untouched. He walked out of the university like a zombie. The next day there was a furore in class. The news of Shuvo's proposal was all over the place. Some sympathising friends came up to him.

'Don't you know she's engaged to Sudip?'

'To Sudip?' It was a thunderbolt. Then the eyes, the deep purple, the ripple he had seen were for someone else! What a fool he was! Friends joked, laughed and tortured him. He felt slighted, his heart withering inside him. The jasmine fragrance of youth was gone. He didn't talk to her again.

After all these years he had seen her! So eager so cheerful! It was as if the very vestige of the day of proposal had vanished from her memory! They were to meet that evening. Shuvo calmed himself. Sundown was a long way off. He went back to bed. But sleep wouldn't come. Restive, anxious and apprehensive, he reprimanded himself. Still the same; outwardly placid, inwardly restless Shuvo. The passion that was lurking all these years was scouring all over him now, in spite of the insult, the ignominy and pain. The layered decade couldn't quell the dancing breeze on the gold-green grass of his emotions. Nothing changed. The same flutter was resurrected the day he met her. He hated himself.

They met. Talked of the past. On her cheek appeared the pink; so dear to him once.

'Shuvo, don't talk to me of that day in the canteen! Please! I'm thoroughly ashamed of what I said to you!'

'No, you shouldn't be. I was a fool to believe, what I believed then!'

'Let's forgive and forget. Let us be friends again,' she answered.

'Oh yes. Of course!'

Mita was unusually frank with Shuvo. The latter was cautious. They had only met twice. She was so voluble!

'Sudip jilted me-.'

'Why?' he asked.

'I really don't know. To think how I behaved with you—just because of him!'

'Leave those matters of the past alone, Mita.'

'Yes, but the incident had been haunting me ever since I met you.'

'Then whom did you marry?' he veered the topic.

'A doctor—a rake, a drunkard; used to torture me physically. Left him after six months. I'm happy as I am.'

Mita went home invigorated by the tête-à-tête. It seemed to her that she had crossed the last impediment that hindered her passageway of life. It was a destination she should arrive at before it was too late. Her heart swelled with expectation of a reach. The nemesis for mistaking a diamond for a piece of glass was over.

They met oftener, even thrice a week, taking trips to various places— eating out, spending whole days together. Shuvo could discern the ripples in the depths of her eyes again;—this time it was for him he knew. Her shoulders often brushed his—, her fingers lightly and delightfully came closer—his arms were around her, when she accidentally slipped— steadying her firmly, assuringly. He was impeccable in his behaviour towards her. Outwardly, unperturbed. But he was always like that; Mita thought. His rectitude was unquestionable.

Days passed, months elapsed. Shuvo was cool. Sometimes she detected a tremulousness in his voice, the dark, deep huskiness, speaking of pent-up ardour of years, which he was afraid to reveal. He had every right to conceal his sentiments she thought, considering his first experience. For her, the relationship was new. She let herself go into the pristine tides of bitter-sweet surprises; diving deep with elation in the discovery of what Shuvo really was. She was suffused with the warmth and sincerity of the man she was once stupid enough to reject. To her, it was not only a resurrection of those vibes she once had for Sudip, but a submersion in the wealth of affections she had never felt so intensely for anyone, not even Sudip. Mita gloried in the thought of his proximity. His breath on her shoulders sent messages that made her nights restless with exhilaration. She loved him, she was delirious with joy when he was with her; his eyes deeply intent, searching her. She had at last found her man.

Mita decided to propose. It was her fault the first time; she decided to make amends by initiating it.

As they sat in the coffee-shop Shuvo observed the colour rise on her cheeks. He knew that the moment had come. He had rehearsed every word again and again for this moment. Mita observed his contentment. He had remained a bachelor for her only, she knew. He was too emotional to speak. He ordered coffee and gave her an encouraging smile, to put her at ease. Silence was penetrating. The coffee was served. Minutes went by, both were reticent. Then Mita held Shuvo's hand and said, 'I love you Shuvo, with my heart and soul, I want you to marry me.'

Shuvo did not disengage his hand. There was a trace of a smile which exuded requital. Slowly, his eyes became misty. Mita's cheeks were burning crimson. He didn't respond, but took his time.

'Shuvo what's the matter?' She was impatient.

'Mita it's too late for that. Friendship? Yes. But, ...

PART II

POEMS

GODDESSES

Inside a brick construct, darkness
Smothers dark.
A scented paddy field of unripe years,
Overwhelmed by stench of putrid game
Stories of redness on green—unfold.
The hot virgin sky flushes out shades of crimson
Sunnily malignant on burial grounds
Of screams—throttled by lust of centuries.
Torn legs, slit throats—run through the centre
Of the city. Beastly propriety
Demands, 'Do not unclothe before devouring.'
A car moves, cigarette smoke, heads jostled—
The crying earth receives—a kick-out,
Lacerated, worm eaten—a no-body-a lady said,
'No character'—nothing to think about.
The woman on the tower roars—
No, no, contrived—The woman with a whip
Chides, go, Honest, go—where truths are told—
Then no screens—that face—many faces
Mingled thousands,—'No, no, not anymore—'
Why do we worship clay goddesses!
The cycle begins again.

CONTRARY SPIRIT

Billion stars etch your name
In cosmic turbulences of surreal lights
Igniting a solitary fire in the lonely portal
Of my heart, demanding a song.
I try chanting by rote the lines forefathers set
Humbled by your terrible force.
But Om Shantih! escapes;—a nowhere
My lips voicing aspirant fears
In the horrid circle of death.

As I join my hands in supplication
My brain erupts in contrary madness.
The pain, this fever, your radiance denies
Those microcosmic dreads inflated
Ripping the loins of the earth
To nether spheres.

Yet I know your kisses,
Drops of dew on dawn-stirred trees,
Migrating birds and baby-stirring wombs;
On dry leaves on torrid zones,
But empty-bowl screech millions,
Virgin red in monster carpets, killer drones
Can't define my heart—your own.

CITYSCAPE

It has to be good-bye.
The colours I had seen before
Fly in dust coated monotone.
In my youth I had dipped those red-pink hues
In pristine greens, the beaks knocking the windows
Till I answered their calls.
The barks rarely visited now—
Their grey bodies stand waiting the impending
Doom, in glittering high-rises.
I cannot see the moon; the slatey clouds burdened,
Float haltingly, not white frigates on the azure sky
But frightened of jostling towers,
Burying the moist earth.

The lotus pond gets a befitting farewell.
Tadpoles, radiant fish, snakes and water-babies
Describe stones and bricks, until my sighs grow thick
With venom of ambitious dreads. I choke—
Sandy nightmares throttle me, till I forget
To breathe—
The rain-soaked fragrance of the past.

CARELESS

You dust the dreams off my shoulders
Peppering them with chips of stone,
Rusty chests creak open and distances
Create arid pastures, I had left alone.
The smiles fabricate useless jokes
Masking the irritable, your lips connive
To deceive the time.

There will be a moment when washed
Walls will be riddled with scars of the past—
Denting into soured fragrances
In your room; grizzled and withered
Faces, mirror the rushing
Of what's to follow soon.

I'll watch excited, my boiling interiors
Still meriting the wait, my heart
Of sand and earth lying still straight
As before, as countless stars pass by—
Night-drenched visions a girl once had,
And perseverance, till she is no longer old
But metamorphosing—a child of a girl
Who no longer cares whether hearts
Are made of bricks and stones, whether
A bird which flew past, grew
On a rugged tree, beating its wings.

AFGHAN SOLILOQUIES

1979

They took me out
Pushed me to the edge
Of a cliff
Gagged and tied.
That night they stormed
With war-planes
Found my hideout,
Razed my hut
And killed my sons.
Hoped to be free
But still I hear
The Soviet cannons gun—

1998

I was terrified.
Souls banging on unfortified bodies
Bowing low to religious lies
Force me kneel and pray
In obeisance
To wishes.
War declared
On kind.
They'll wage war
In another name
At another time.

Victim of the mountains, my clan
They hanged me long ago
To purge sins
Off a holy land.

2001

I'm born time and again, to die
Feel, pain of loss
Once more
What seemed to be mine.
As I lie—
My wounds imbibe
Hankerings of the dead
Spirits chained in mountains
And mysteries shed—
See my wife
Cross thresholds
Fascinating sparks on gloom
Crossing towards garden twilight—
See U.S. warplanes zoom
A flash in the sky
Next minute
Vibrations
Smother a twilight cry.

Around me shadows lengthen
In mute complaint
Against laws
Meant to be broken.
I'm silent.
Never dared learn
'Terror begets terror'
Blame none
For this.
It's Him
It's Him
I whisper.
Was it cowardice

Praying, to revoke
Once at least
The catastrophe?
The prayer was never meant to be
Unanswered.

At last I wait in line
To taste
Franchise.
Darkness underneath
Darkness outside.
I have discovered
My child
Lying still and cold
Right by my side.

THE OTHER SIDE OF DARKNESS

'VICTORY'
She pulls it on a leash.
Head down, apprehending new terrors
He crawls, shamed to obeisance.
'Bark', she says, 'bark'.

Mouth opens, collar hurts.
'Bark, dog!' She repeats.
He tries, but tears, not shadows
That once unsighted him, fills his eyes.
Can dog cry?
Freedom sits weary on the other side of
midnight.
She laughs, drags the tether, face lighted
By scent of spoil,
'This for the President'.
Cigarette on mouth, her fingers high-rise
The 'V'sign'. Jubilations all around.
Other voices behind, dark and hushed
The rest crushed hard under rifle butts.

'Victory'—a click.
Capped heads, uniforms, mouth agape—
Things to have fun with in a dry state.
Build pyramids, not a novelty
Yet proven records show, humiliation
Not even third degree
Could be excitingly effective
On these darkies—these infidels, these savages!
She snaps open trousers, freedom hangs its head.
'Let's give them what they want.'
Build pyramids
With arms, hands, scrotums, legs,
One on top of the other
Flesh on flesh, flesh on flesh.
She pants with dark thrills
On the pile of exuding maleness. Bonfire burns,
Cups frothing, excitement passes around.
Incredible sight!
Strong men, naked, screwed up, bent
Sized-up with taunts, piled, arranged
A jigsaw puzzle—A droll.
Giggles, giggles, giggles. Capped heads roll.
Tickles between legs.
'Can't find whose feet, whose hands, whose head!'
Garbaged, naked flesh, life's spill-overs,
Inflamed putrescence,
Festered wounds sprouting
On freedom's catacomb;
On humiliation of obedience.
'Let's build more pyramids. Remember,
We the Pharaohs—undead'.

Pain shifts regularly, one to the other side
East to west to east to west.
Freeze-shots on bruises.
Years pass, ashes pile high—
On Vietnam—
Interpreting blurred divide—
The right and the wrong
Of shaded blacks from the white monotone
Of who symbolizes what!
Equations aren't muddled yet
Everyone knows—,
Who are so proud to be civilised
And who are not!

All along, the wily strumpet sleeps
Closing doors and windows.
White dreams on a white bed.
'Washington' she awakes and says,
'Is coming tonight.'
She steps down, rubs her shoes hard
On the jet black door mat
And smiles.

Note: On the inhuman treatment of Iraqi prisoners-of-war by American soldiers in Abu Gharib and other prisons.

SCHOOLING HIGH, IN BESLAN

Georgy, here's your ball, your car and your teddy bear.
I've put out all the lace
To cover—
There isn't any left in the house.
But I just couldn't wipe that thing off your face, my sweetie
So scared was I of hurting you more.
Anna too, didn't.
She said, she'd rather try putting inside
Vera's, favourite doll—
Couldn't see her face though—
And Eva's six-month old's matted hair
Left as it is.
I keep asking everyone, who is it next?
Who else is going?
My neighbours don't look up—

And little Katerina who comes to play
With Georgy everyday
Is looking so lovely in her white dress
(Though none can see her little hands)
That everyone has started to cry.
I keep staring at Georgy's face.
Don't know I waited days
The gunshots, screams, gay ribbons
Turned red—
And more than three hundred
Stretched out, and the rest—
I just can't remember.

Three hundred bodies lying,
Studying terror first-hand
And with them, attending class
My little Georgy!

Sweetheart, before you go
I mustn't forget the milk bottle
Anyway, you can't go to sleep hungry;
Your face pressed so tight to my breast!

No, no, no, no,—
Why can't I find the flower
Matching the red on your lips?

Note: Incident of Chechen terrorism in 2004 where more than 300
Russians including men, women and children were killed when they tried
to escape from a school in Beslan where they were held captive. Even
six-month old children were not spared.

<u>KNOWLEDGE</u>

At a point I silence questions.
Not a highway to eternity I know
But a blind alley constricting
To push out distant answers.
Only stench of drains
And rooftops squaring the sky
Hide what is left of us.

Yet there was a time
When your eyes could hold
Chronicles of wind and rain
When the earth was soft
In you and me.

Now we debate on deeds
Dry and old; to consume what remains
In memory; the footprints
Once converged on a path of light—
For shadows; to dissect
And understand.

CLASSROOM

The bottled sun trickles
Through bars, describing
A ribbed morning; a diluted
Milk-glass beam which sports
No creamy edges to sharp
Corridor points into classrooms.
Waiting, waiting—for shells
To burst, no frothing lips
Curled red, or brown, or edges
Of cropped hair—nothing—
Empty screaming laments the void.
In the large staff-lounge
New ambitions cackle
Gulling vociferous over dead shoals
On dry beaches—the knowing old
Corner-cringed and slit-brow-rings
Meditate on what's left of tomorrow.

DEMENTIA

Between the drowsy smoke of oblivion and remembrance
The pampering zone of twilight looms.
A glint on the purple stream—a fade in—
And then a no more.
In the cool evenings revolutions disturb,
Turning sepia to colour—eyes wayward
Don't define green fields so near;
Vapourising; leaving distant blur.
Names trick; jumbled card games
But childhood rhymes tease my brain.
The swirling, surfing on rising tides,
Then floating frames of blue and green
Father's glistening whip, the dust tracks
Of cartwheels, a garden hoe, a whiff of scent
And warmth of mother's breast.

A sea of faces, a sea of faces
Undulating around—
To me—nothing.

SENILITY

It's not just writing names on walls
For everything passes out of sight into night-space
The hollow breath; a whistle only
Into feverish times
Melts like printed letters on an empty page.

Incidents are but dents in memory
Pushing into moments of fluid stretch
Along coastal shores at night
When age sits and broods at cross-roads;
When expected night-shrieks of birds
Wake up the putrid scent of flesh
Borne along waste of city lights in gathering dusk
The rolling tin cans discarded on dusty side-walks
Whisper what remains of cluttered words
Dropped ages ago or retracing footsteps
Fading into chaos in front; and the rest—
Just an empty space.

AT THE STATION

. . . and afterwards I'll sit, watching on a rusty bench
Colours peeling off walls
In an abandoned waiting-room.
I'll stare at time-charts in yesterday's frames,
The tickings, to cheat farewells in interspaces
Of speech and pain,
So that wind may come inside to stir the rust
Off hinges, along with the fading din of wheels
Set to usher the darkness in,
The whistle to blow, shadows to rise
For me, to begin again.

KALI

The dark deep of your cosmic fury
Enhances the menace of your stare
And thousands of nights in eternal whirlwind
Unwind the splendour of your hair.
Oh ruthless Mother! Monster heads hang on your grip,
Oh! Mad Goddess of blood and gore,
Rush your strike—the lightning of your armour
Thunders with murderous roar; the cleansing continues—
Oh! Darkest of the dark, soul of souls
The love that burns your heart
With raging fires; look inside the earth,
Your milk-filled tenderness cries
But you rise in oblivion of the softer calls
And avoid; pulverising each demonic bubble
You, mother eagle with claws poised
Ready to strike—!
Oh! Goddess, your unmeasured steps nonchalant,
Halts at last in tongue-protruded shame,
Shiva, the lord of life claims your feet
To restrain; your crazy dance of death.

Oh! Mother regain, regain your dark beauty
Take us in your arms
To taste
The milk of peacefulness.

KRISHNA

In a corner of a room, I wait in prayers,
Searching for answers to the creative vortex,
The circular turbulence, defying void.
I don't rotate in hymnal dance
But when I look at you
My heart is cooled by the flavour of your glance.

Oh! Krishna, Are you the chariot-driver
Driving Arjuna to destiny?
One to whom, the secrets of the world unveiled—,
The one of cosmic fury?
Your thousand blazing jaws; the rush of death—
Heads and torsos in the tremendous holocaust,
The cavernous mouth—an eternity—
Holding gushing oceans, stars innumerable
And the dead undead, the undead dead
All fated to be engulfed, by the sweeping will
Of your imperial force!

My dearest lord, I cannot find you there
I look for your flute-playing pranks
Your Radha, your gopis, your herd, your friends!
Come, distilled of terrible remembrance.
Come in innocence; crawl; so
I can hold you to my breast
And say, 'I love you my dearest.'

THE JUST

We keep on asking why
Your insatiable rage
Rips the veil off an incredulous world
Silencing questions.
Terror follows terror
Untimely remonstrances in a million quakes
Overturn sanity of earth; unguarded,
Naked, vulnerable
Feeding your malice.

Smiling in brilliant insouciance
Your dice dances on chequered boards of destiny,
Yet each violence understands
Only belief—and blind homage;
For purposeful destination of future victims.

You play truant
Shuffling underwater plates,
Playing apocalypse with elements—
Your cosmic fury
Metamorphosing civilized history
Into holocaust
Stretching even more
Through bleeding centuries of dust.

In the sanctum sanctorum
Myths of incense still rise,
Prayers chanted.

LINES ON AN ABANDONED GIRL-CHILD

Waters break.
I crack up
A cloudy sky
Discharging dust
On hot fluid;
Messages that wake up
Indifferent joys
Rolled along tubular by-lanes
Blood, eggs, bones, cells,
A concerted quest
Breathing into nothingness—,
And to disgorge secretly
On dark nights,
Dark lanes.

My cave is of full moons
Pushing out aspiring suns
Breaking dark red
In embryonic patterns; ribboned cells
Floating on turgid waters
Inside the catacomb.
Each year reminds me
Of a distant sun
Mourning a blasted womb
Scarred and scared
Of lunar births.

I scream, push against walls
In me, milk and honey
Turning to gall
Wrenching the thing off—
A shriek—
Moon slips off a contorted tree
Again.
I'll not see that face.
I'll not cry.
My breasts are mountains—
My eyes, two discs in curtains.
Don't chant verses on me.
The eclipse begins.

The night is a slithering cheat.
Does innocence throb tender-?
Cut the cackle.
Loveliness devours, disarms.
Wrap her.
Unsheathe urges, hard steel, razor sharp.
Discard on city lanes.
Stray dogs watch over
Ragged dolls in drains—

In dreams they come and go
Hiding sins
We choose not to know.

SUMMER

White heat of noon pierced by hiss of curtailed breath,
On the streets wasted remains of flesh
Is burnt to cinders. None to account
Loss under small awnings when roads are bare—
The slivered day, diced smaller into nothingness—
No not a footstep—but in the still heat
Huddled under trembling skyscrapers
The voice of a child.

Hushed inside A.C. rooms
Lies the stretched out bust of a mad city,
Cold drinks and softer zones-allude—
Evening promenades or coffee—.
Resting on heated lanes and carting roads
Trundling the screech of pain in melting dents of tar
Footfalls print the weary silence
Of limbs that refuse to go thus far—
And yet, return again and again
To another explosion of day—
Scripting pages of loss or gain
Another scorched season of uncomplaint
To the melting heat of a cruel sky.

POETIC FAILURE

Each moment I sketch
Words with fire
Feeding endlessly on winds
That blow in my ribs—
From time to time.
Words, sun-drenched or rain-wet,
Rainbow colours and grey-white
Flirt on the landscape of my eyes.

I can't step out—but within myself
Watch, words take form
And run to wilderness, or chaotic storms
Stirring in my womb and in bubbling foam
Of unorganised consciousness.

I stand back, wait—
Expecting a march of words
From upper hemispheres—
Marshalled and sliced by reason
With decided logic supporting the rear.

But I, poor, weak and plain
Can't stop dancing inside—
With promptings of wind and rain.

POISONED FLAVOURS

When loneliness interferes
With felt apprehensions
Redoubling dark shades
Of forest growths on dubious soils
I look for sunlight clearings
To stretch my tired soul.

It is a time when love questions.
A time when answers are not
Sweet to taste.
To introspect, is drinking
Bitter flavours,-dangerous herbs,
Strange and poisonous flowers
Spreading on abandoned graves.

I had stumbled
On the harshness of expectations—
Mistaking noise to music
For half my soul to dance—
But it's only a barren track
That warns—
The moment has come
To distinguish freak hours of joy
Structured to fill vacant moods
And to ease out—
Is drinking gall
The foolish frailty of belief—
That it isn't
A game at all!

WISH I KNEW

It took you seconds
To conquer the sea.
Diving down and tasting
The warm wet lunacy
I thought took you in so—
It was only make believe, how could I know!
For me, yours was just a hunch
Sweating madly to escape time's jostle
And dance in the open—a sprightly dance
Trampling doubts—
Have I really found it out?
The secret prattling on magical evenings
On opposite sides. Tell me,
I'll hold my breath—
If not, keep still, open your eyes
Let looks do the rest—
I'll not complain
Against a mesmerising death.

LAST THOUGHTS OF A DYING PROSTITUTE

Winter has been kind to me.
The mist settled at last.
Two scratched discs
Watched mysteries of night hauled out,
Now in cover.
Sixty years—. Bottled fire
Poured down blackened holes—
Lees of lust cemented; the smell
Escapes in quiet spurts.
Calm closure of cap.
Unlike last groans of salvation-seekers!
Sly hypocrites!
But ends; so ordinary. Flowers,
Prescribed sympathies, oblivion.
Glad I don't see pictures of gods.
Don't want crowds.
Trampled footprints
On yesterday's rib-cage
Oppress me.
This winter is best.
None but the cat—
A trail of blood
Lining slashed veins
Of battered past
That runs amok
Grey loins

Of my grisly courtyard
Now under
Yellow leaves and mud
Burying sins
Of an insouciant world.

EXAM HOUR

The swish of pens scratch silence.
Beyond colours of youthful meditation
Ripples of delight arrive.
A bird, black and white
Steps on the window sill.
Heads are bent
Word-devoured minds
Oblivious of magic at the rear.
It turns its tail
Moments a jig, then flies
On top of a branch
Cleaning, shaking dust off wings.
The flapping erases
Dull stagnancy of time
Until it disappears—
And once again the scrawls
Remind me of the exam hour.

REMAINS OF DAY

I'm digging incessantly.
The sun scorches me.
All I discover in sweat
Is nothing but the rotting garbage
Of days' flesh.
Heart steeled, my loins ache
With the burden of fever
Of generations in vortex.
I try finding a place
To plant a tree—
Working away at another hole.
But bones and powdered toil
Of millions invade—
Waking up
Soil-pasted civilizations
Counting doomsday.

EXPECTATIONS

Let the sea draw back and show
The greater length of its wisdom
To let us walk hand in hand
Before the sand drinks up
The language of love—
On the exposed shores that lie await,
When time will call and I will say,
'I gave you the sea—I gave you the shore'
And with tearless eyes,
I'll let you go.

RENDEZVOUS

I walk the backstreets of life
Alone, in dimly lit passages
Roaring and slithering; sidewalks
Escaping into chaos of night.

Metallic walls, lined faces
Like shadows of disembodied thoughts—
Spectres; wandering past cobbled streets,
Cantering—breaking silent heights.

I hoped to decentralise, merge,
Roll inside the accumulated dark
Crying in me inconsolably.

With all my cravings I hoped
It would be a recession
A dissolution, till I found words
Lighted within the depths of my troubled soul
To realise, drown in, unwind.
But suddenly you came along
Came in twilight, bearing a song.

THE OTHER

You roam
Wilds of reckless fancies
My frenzied recap
Of your insouciance
Culminating in painful; a stretch
Rigid with askance.

Trembling days
Anticipate thrills of meets
Till ecstasies swallow
Each retreating foot.

Seeing you is holding
Myriad dreams; floating along
With scraps of consciousness
Each day; a transcendence—
Brooding over declining to-morrows
And myths of yesterdays.

I smell in flowers
Your breath; in minutest throbs
Of passing nights—
And prayers navigated
Along thirsty lanes
Screaming silently through time.

Your echoes magnify
Whispers of ancients
In porticos and halls
Long abandoned cities, waking up
To surface—the long lost.

You evoke
Wide open corridors
Strange, measureless expanse
Microscoping yet
Domestic pieties; allegiance.

Dawn dissolves to poetry
Your eyes relish
Images I wish to see
But shadows intervene
Walls in a torched city.
The yearning darkens
Pregnant with surmise
Not at odds with eternity
Spasms of time—
With drift of evenings
Each pain commands
The wait, the yearning
Till the finishing line.

AFTERTHOUGHTS

The anguish rearranging itself
Settles in reams of evening mists
Spilling over forbidden walls
That line the reach between
You and me.

I shoulder the cross;
Walking the corridors of chartered thoughts,
Avoiding the chinks
Broken bits, that let the sunlight in—
Atoms filtering, focus on the outer being—
Your face, masked and grim
Reluctant, never free
Even to look at me.

The measured rain-walk,
The breezed refrain,
Roadside pub's heat
Melt into distant aches.
I try to trap the living light of your eyes
Before it vanishes
And time comes to begin again.

When in whim of evenings.
You sprawl, callous—
I play games of shadows
Rising and falling—
Trace waves, cutting across
Your formal face
Stretched—timeless.

Then I suddenly remember
The voiceless pang straightens up
Prompting you to grasp my hand
In drowning seas—,
Breaking shackles—
Hear you shake silence
In reprimands—
Then—I understand.

<u>RECONCILIATION</u>

I can read thunderstorms.
The season's burst of moods
Such as when sparrows brood
Over mountains of mist—
Or dust sweeps through carpets of green.

Your nostrils twitch and eyelids bat
Making claims of stormy monsoons
Deep in my heart
When the wet crow shivers
Weighed down with moistened wings
That I embark—
On a dangerous journey of wind and rain.

Yet this time of year comes
In the swelling heat of mangoes
Invisible ripenings registered
On empty tracts of absence.
Soft footfalls on patient time
When buds grow hankering for form
Sweetened fires encouraging
Forgetfulness of the 'other' season.

Summer is not a myth, nor unseasonal spring
When autumn vanishes shivering
And storms at last decide
To wake sleepy oceans
With ravishing tides.

COCKROACH

I was too young to know
Whether I loved you
So I thought introduction might help
Though hating the way cockroaches
Were beaten down with brooms
(A clean-up drive before expected arrival)
When they tried climbing walls and flew
Knocking themselves down outside our doors
And the glee with which bodies were counted;
One, two, three, four—
Laid on a heap
A mangled mess of wings and needle-legs
I shuddered and thought I'd flee—
They did it according to plan.
Dinners, parties, introductions
Then the final countdown.
(What a romantic view of escape!)
Till that night I saw you on the bed
Searching inside closed doors
Your eyes, torches,
Determined to 'find out.'
Then I discovered suddenly
Who was 'it'
Quaking inside a box.

NOSTALGIA

If you want, stretch your soul
To the wonder of discovery
On a lighted portico or hall
When the wind will rattle your palace door
Telling how we walked history
Making melodious space,
Bonfires in poetry, and
Those days when all the clocks
Of this world failed to tick.

Alarming stones were passed by
Each snap stowed away with dusty breaths
Sticking in interspaces of 'said' and 'unsaid'
But now dead words survive
In the closed albums of life.
Gradually a shelved destination—
Looking out, passing stations—
And then vapours rise.

Another journey will soon begin
A discovery then, at cross-roads
Trying hard to pull—the thread
Of remembrance—
Your query who I am
I, the same in return,
Bridges will be crossed.
You'll turn your back
And I'll let you go.

THE DIVIDING LINE

In the fag
Little is left for ashes.
Leftovers in the meal of life
Turn mouldy
With perennial clock-ticks
And class-over bells.
Why this agony
At the end of the waiting line
Or intermittent cut-shorts
To describe havoc in lust,
Curtailed greed; wine-frost—
All this for crying-zone
A short dividing line
A here and a no more.

MY CITY, MY LOVE

Each event is just a quiver
In the matrix of pain.
Processions hog the limelight
Handouts screeching political gains
Choke traffic at rush hours.
I stand deaf to the sound of wind and rain
Stare blankly; crowds pass by
Cross avenues of defeat;
Pooled in garbage and drains
City patterns contour disease
In coughed up men
Children spawned on polythene sheets
Holed too big, zooming in eyes
Eager to release tented secrets
On dusty urban roads.

I watch innocence of one minute ecstasies
Grow skilled in deceit; traded, trained
For survival games, scavenging
With street-dogs
Still dewy eyed, still smiling
On refusal at cross-roads.
Unicef babies naked in the winter rain
Spark fireworks in aristo-political terrains
Conference five hours,
Five inter-dinner halls
Prolong, philanthropic pain
Eased in evening

Desires delicately poised, let grow
In heat of discotheque fires.
Do I measure steps at night?
Chess-board back-streets where pawn men wait
Bleary eyed, baited junk
On sleepless foot-paths;
Jobless fantasies slithering at dusk
Disappearing with city freaks
In dark, slimy, gliding side-walks,
Stalking nameless open armed terror
Promising death to hot-seats
The more bloody; the bloodier treats.

I bear the city-shame
Chequered lights spot on
Tipsy, indolent men,
Fed by hungry wives, worn-out, work-bent,
Women thrashed, flogged
Pushed down again and again
Overriding jockeys in uniforms,
Faceless faces, ten, twenty, thirty—
Shadows of dusk unite
Drawn to a single combat
One, another, then another—
Crush, deflower, drive
In the power's name.
All deftly trained to cork shrieks
One dead stroke—
An easy game.
I'm never shocked, not ashamed
I don't cry,
I have become
One of them.

ETERNAL

If you feel free to let me define
Dreams for us—
Stretch out; wait
On a roadside pub, Italy
When melting light
Dances to evenings, roseate
In champagne glasses—
Or leaping Vesuvius, to drown
In Capri's red-gold sea.

Imagine the night lend a hand
To sands, burnt out—
Settle over mists rearranging
The distant waters of your eyes
When calling me—
Mask discarded;
You wait.

Let's watch beneath
Stars shooting dark, sky to sky,
Your fireside breath
Melting me . . .
The surge of salted sea-tide
Leaping to touch in flames
Each flitting light
Dancing down
In the deeps of your eyes.
Feel nightsweat

Drench folds of desire
With a rose-blush; setting fire
To your arms, encircling
The space of my dreams
To die; before the trance is over.

We'll roam lost kingdoms, vast ruins,
Crumbling amphitheatres—;
Of royal blood
Spilled offstage; in the
Annals of Grecian art.
Million eyes . . . . and
Mighty souls dressed for death to the quick,
The fatal good-byes.

Is it you and I
Have tread a thousand times
Same tracts, the same old lands
In drawing room corners, breeding shadows
Reincarnated . . .
Deleted, born again
Centuries floating, rehearse the pain
With you and me at crossroads.

Ever felt the same?

THE UNKNOWN

I don't understand why doodles upset me.
In the still darkness of my unnamed self
I mistake figures that make meanings
In black and white; yet in spite of the insensible
Credulity of living a well-rehearsed life
The over-boundaries threaten me with thunderstorms.
On the table an unread book, a focus on the dangerous
Chapters of mist, I avoid consciously, though curtains flap
In the wind, a wake-up call, to unroll
The secret river inside
The hungry receptors of my brain.

I am careful to carry a hood, to ward off
Undisturbingly disturbing calls: yet head
To the terrace to seek out what remains sensible
Beyond the parameters of time
The criss-crossing of shadows, a burst of air,
Chills the advocacy of reason
I wait, I wait for the moment to come.

THE ALIEN

Curtains flap. The wind whistles hard
flirting with time-charts
while inside you creepers connive
how to serialise in the dark—
hollow names.
The sudden kill flattens you, knocking out
your senses, before you're ready to face
what mirrors hide.
You picture coloured fabrics in neighbours' rooms
and think of lurking bed-time shadows
in the dark, or the nearby water-pumps
vociferous with the thirst of people in glass-houses
awashed by the gurgly stream
rehearsing reasons to live,
rehearsing reasons to give.
On a nearby tree, birds break into a menacing cackle
tearing the vacuum.
Here, drips of there and then
float in flash-backs
of how your hair grew grey with trust
each a date with memory
how you cheated the clocks, to love,
how answered to knocks
plundering the calls of your heart.
Yet the years winking, betrayed
nothing but the ebb—
the sketch-book of reason
circling the final countdown—